Six-Gun Atonement

Six-Gun Atonement

LAURAN PAINE

Sagebrush
Large Print Westerns

Library of Congress Cataloging in Publication Data

Paine, Lauran.
   Six-gun atonement / Lauran Paine.
     p.   cm.
   ISBN 1-57490-148-6 (hardcover : alk. paper)
   1. Large type books. I. Title.
   [PS3566.A34S54 1998]
   813'.54—dc21   98-8375
                                                       CIP

Cataloguing in Publication Data is available from
the British Library and the National Library of Australia.

Sagebrush Large Print Westerns are published in the United
States and Canada by Thomas T. Beeler, Publisher, Box 659,
Hampton Falls, New Hampshire 03844-0659. ISBN 1-57490-148-6

Published in the United Kingdom, Eire, and the Republic of South
Africa by Isis Publishing Ltd, 7 Centremead, Osney Mead, Oxford
OX2 0ES England. ISBN 0-7531-5906-6

Published in Australia and New Zealand by Australian Large Print
Audio & Video Pty Ltd, 17 Mohr Street, Tullamarine, Victoria, 3043,
Australia. ISBN 1-86442-254-8

Manufactured in the United States of America by BookCrafters, Inc.

CHAPTER ONE

IT WAS THE SMELL OF SWEAT, HE THOUGHT. MAYBE not altogether that, but it must be a part of it. Anyway, he was losing her. She was drifting away as surely as the sunset over the far mountains that stuck up like Spanish bayonets or crooked fingers, reaching for the sky.

A mighty man with features battered with the passage of time, blasted out of life by experiences that were rarely pleasant. Corded with muscles packed under a tawny hide of sunblasted health. Troy Muller was a blacksmith in the cowtown of Bannock. A man who invariably smelt of cinders, and—worse—the strong odor of horses; always. A hard working man with a gentle heart and passive mind where Cin was concerned. It had been like that for six idyllic years, but gradually he had sensed that the plating was wearing off, ever so gradually, so gently and cooly, but definitely wearing off. At first there was a dumb uneasiness, like an oxen might feel. Then there was something akin to panic, fright, desperation—the terrible loneliness that was coming toward him inexorably and inevitably. And it worked a miracle in chemicals, too, because Troy Muller himself, was changing. Throwing up a defensive mechanism inside his soul to protect himself.

He went into the little house and smelled her perfume. The reaction had always been the same. A delicious sickness in his chest—and an idea that she used so much to offset the less pleasant odor that clung to him; to the blacksmith who made good money, owned his own shop, and had the perpetually opened pores and eager

1

sweat of his tribe.

"Cin?"

She came from the direction of the kitchen. A woman with level gray eyes, a beautiful, sensuous mouth and a thin nose. A woman of breeding that had taken generations to make, and also a woman with ambition enough for three sisters—and no conscience at all, or, if she had one, it was chilled by the lack of passion in the icy blood she had.

She held out the stein of beer he always wanted when he got home, saying nothing. The gray eyes went over him with the same look they always had. Admiration for his powerful, thick chest, shoulders and arms, and a bitter dash of disdain for the use he made of them.

He took the beer and held it. The sensation was thicker than ever in the room with them. She stood just under the hanging braids of knots, garnished with long glass beads, he had made for the partition between the small parlor and the smaller dining room. It wasn't hard to understand his almost infantile need for her. She radiated strength, intelligence and ambition. She also gave out a sense of magnificent fertility; abundance and more, that actually was camouflage because she was cold, but Nature had made her that way.

Cynthia understood this now, at twenty-eight, where at twenty it had bewildered her, even frightened her somewhat, until the years and Troy Muller had taught her why men regarded her like that.

"Thanks," he said, making no move to drink the beer. Looking at her because she was the only thing he'd seen in twelve hours that didn't have a beard, smoke strong tobacco, chew and spit where he had to lay his tools, or just plain talk horses.

She smiled slightly. Just a parting of the heavy lips to

show perfect teeth beneath. An acknowledging smile and nothing else. The kind that could mean everything—or nothing.

"You ready to eat?"

He nodded without hearing. Like music it was. Soft, sensual music. As different from a shoe being hammered on an anvil or the throaty cursing of men, as night from day.

"I reckon. Soon's I clean up."

She turned away then, letting her answer ride the slipstream that came back over one shoulder when she headed back toward the kitchen.

"Hurry up. It's all ready."

He looked down at the beer, smelled its richness and drank it off, put the glass down on the rubber plant canister just inside the door—something he'd never done before—swore to himself and hiked for the back porch where a basin of lukewarm water awaited him, lye soap, and a towel suspended by a nail. There was something moving in the background of his brown eyes. Coiled and writhing and sort of like desperation.

A person who knew the Bannock blacksmith well enough—and few did—could have guessed that something was changing inside of him. The passiveness, the slow, torpid bullishness was losing ground before an onslaught of something like desperation. But a man like Troy was taken for granted always. Big and patient and stolid. He had to be that way because everyone knew those great hulks were always like that. He was a type, and everyone knew types were—well—like that. Whoever heard of a feisty giant or a stolid little man?

The meal was nearly over in silence when Troy made an effort. He saw the ennui in Cin's eyes and, lacking understanding of it, nevertheless tried to break it.

3

"Sold that new dealer at the Palace a Tipton buggy today. Real nice, with a fringed top and all."

The stolidness disappeared but nothing pleasant replaced it. Her gray, large eyes pinioned him for a second before she spoke. With no knowledge of women to speak of, Troy nevertheless, intuitively, knew what was behind her words—in her thoughts.

"Now he can drive around like a gentleman, can't he?"

He nodded, eating again and willing for the dull silence to come back. It did.

The same thing happened at bedtime. Another effort to scale the wall of inertia that surrounded her.

"They say Jeb Carter's in the country again."

"Who told you that?" It was almost a challenge.

He shrugged, forcing his eyes off her, trying to act the indifference he certainly didn't feel. "Sheriff. Tom Buffum. He came into the shop for a reset this afternoon. Just gossiping, him and me. Said Carter's got more wanted bills on him now than any other outlaw in Arizona. Totals somewhere around ten-thousand dollars."

Cin laid her bathrobe across the foot of the bed and tried to make herself inconspicuous, avoiding his eyes sullenly, for the second it took to climb between the cotton sheets.

"At least he's made money. Is a success—in his line."

It was a deliberate and successful maneuver Troy—no man—would make advances when his pride had been humbled.

He felt the diminishing ardor and felt resentment taking over in its stead. "I'd rather be shoeing horses and selling a buggy now and then—and be alive, than make Jeb's kind of money and never live to spend it."

"What makes you think he doesn't spend it? Everyone knows he has the best horses, lives high, has all the money he needs."

His head turned a little so he could look at her. "You don't sound like you're ashamed we used to know him."

"I'm not," she fired back. "Why should I be? When he was breaking horses around Bannock he was a nice fellow." She shrugged. "I'm not ashamed I danced with him, either."

Wisely he didn't answer. Instead of breaking down her resistance to him, he was building it higher by going along in the conversation. He lay thoughtfully, long after she blew down the lamp chimney and turned her back to him, sighed and relaxed.

All he knew with any certainty was that she was his life. More than wife, lover, companion. His life. And she was drifting away. Perplexed, he watched the new moon create patterns of cottonwood leaves on the far wall and ceiling, and didn't notice their lacy finery, then he went to sleep.

Troy's burden went with him to the forge. It followed him shadow-like through the days that followed and didn't even leave him when the bearded, handsome man with the ice-water blue eyes and soft, quiet voice rode into the shop from the rear and dismounted, standing close to his horse, studying the two helpers who worked at Muller's Forge.

Troy nodded at the stranger, barely noticing him, looking instead at his horse's hooves. He guessed the animal had been shod no more than two weeks before, and well shod at that although the traits of other smiths he knew around the country weren't evident, then he raised his dark eyes and waited for the stranger to speak.

The man wore two guns, which was unusual but not extraordinary. He was a south-westerner too. It was in the beautiful spade bit, plaited rawhide reins and romal, the slightly oversize saddlehorn and the graceful, Californio spurs on his boots.

The ice-water eyes flickered toward Troy's helpers. Both younger men; he kept one for the forge and anvil work, one for trimming, while he, himself, did the nailing.

"Let 'em have a breather for a-minute."

Troy was startled and showed it. The man wanted to speak to him, but alone. Then he shrugged and called at the workmen and saw them shoot quick, inquisitive glances at the stranger, then stroll out front. This all happened before Troy felt the slight, chilly finger of apprehension.

The two-gun man came forward then, leading the fine black horse and never taking his eyes off Troy's face. "Smith; you like to make fifty dollars, easy and fast?"

Troy blinked, studied the man and gradually felt recognition come into the mind behind his eyes. Jeb Carter! But it was a distinct shock too. He and Cin and even the sheriff, dry, wry, Tom Buffum, had gone to school with the cowboy turned outlaw, killer, stage robber and worse. They had all known him as a likable, headstrong rider in those days. Only three years before at that. But this Jeb Carter was different. He had aged terribly. The beard made him handsome because he had the thin, fine features for it. But there was gray over his ears in payment for the years and hardships, and violence entwined into the courage that lay in his bleak eyes now. More than just the courage of a horsebreaker; the savagery that made brave killers.

"I don't understand you," Troy said, finally, still

6

fascinated by the familiar and strange face.

Carter smiled. It was a quick lifting of the upper lip. A flash of large white teeth in the setting of auburn beard, then it was gone. He moved to one saddle bag, watching Troy over his shoulder as he reached in, pulled something heavy out and hefted it.

"Like this. I got a bar of pure silver here." He laid it on an anvil and smiled again, briefly. "You make it up into four shoes and set 'em on my horse—for fifty dollars."

Troy looked stupidly at the bar of silver. There was something stamped on its face that made him wince. United States Mint—Denver, Colorado. 1886.

Fifty dollars for an hour's work. He thought of the buggy he'd sold the gambler at the Palace Bar across the road, for some inexplicable reason, then his heart thudded into his ribs. With fifty dollars he'd be able to buy, not one just like it, but a better one he had in the corner—with yellow wheels instead of conventional red ones—for Cin.

"All right." He faced the two-gun man gravely. "Carter—you wait out in back."

The blue eyes held unblinkingly to his face. "You got a good memory, Troy."

"No; it isn't that so much." He just shrugged. How could he tell this renegade that his wife had spoken of him a few nights before, saying she was glad she'd danced with him?

Seeing he wasn't going to elaborate, the outlaw nodded at him. "You—you wouldn't get Tom on me, would you Troy?"

He heard the undertone in the words but it didn't frighten him. "No; but you're darned easy to recognize, Jeb. Especially here in Bannock. Out in back and give

7

me an hour."

Carter left and Troy went to work. He sweated copiously, far more than usual and his palms were slippery on the tools. So slippery in fact that he swore lividly twice, and wagged his head to shake off the nervous sweat that ran across the creases in his forehead, gathered at the pinch of his nose and trickled ticklishly down it to drip, one by one, on to the cluttered earthen floor of the shop.

It was a long hour too, because the shop men came back, looked at him oddly and went silently back to their own chores, cleaning up like they always did in between jobs. But he finally finished the horse and took him out the back way. Jeb Carter materialized and made that quick, furtive, unwholesome smile, offering a hand with a thick amount of money in it.

"Fifty, Troy. Count it."

"Get on the horse and go, Jeb. Tom knows you're in the country. He told me so himself a few days back."

Carter nodded speculatively. "Funny, isn't it? How the word gets around. Man can ride in the night, keep out of sight and all, and still word gets around. Beats the hell out of me." He nodded at Troy. "Obliged, oldtimer. Repay the favor someday."

The money was warm in his hand. Troy shook his head quickly, almost savagely. "You owe me nothing."

Jeb Carter turned away, reined the black horse deliberately into a pool of water that leaked around the trough over by the liverybarn next door, and rode north down the back alley.

Troy watched him until he crossed the cluttered, weed choked lot next to Murphy's boarding house and disappeared as he cut into the stage road going gently up the incline out of Bannock. Then he sighed audibly, letting the breath come out slowly, painfully, and pocketed the money without looking down at it, and went back inside, looking at the ground, and sought ways to lose himself in the rush of business.

He drove the yellow wheeled buggy home that night behind the liveryman, Sweeney's, finest chestnut horse, and made Cin a present of it. Now there was surrender, even a responsive fire later, when he touched her.

There was only one ugly scar to the thing, the next day. Sheriff Tom Buffum, his old sweetheart's brother, lounged into the shop and thumbed back his black hat and sat on the only new nail keg in the place where soot hadn't settled. Troy felt his happiness tumble from its high place and lie afraid in the dark recesses of his stomach.

Tom looked at him thoughtfully and smiled. "Blacksmithing's a good business. Wish my back was strong enough to stand it, Troy."

He suspected Tom had seen Cin driving the buggy. It made him feel real guilty again, but he only shrugged. There was a new Troy Muller growing inside the chrysalis. A man willing to fight like a cougar to hold what he wanted. But no one—not even Troy—knew it yet.

"It's hard work, Tom. Not like sheriffing. Lots of sweat to it."

Buffum fished around for his tobacco sack, twisted a cigarette into existence and lit it, exhaling slowly, like a man does who thinks best with tobacco smoke coming out of him.

"Sweat in my business too, Troy. And headaches. I'll show you what I mean." He didn't look at Troy at all when he talked. Just sat on the nail keg relaxed and hump shouldered.

9

"Stage carrying government bullion was robbed over by McKay's cut-off day before yesterday. Feller who done it must've hidden a lot of the loot, but not all of it. It's damned hard to get rid of silver bullion, Troy, and he's figured to have some of it on him.

"Two government men came over from Sante Fe yesterday. The three of us tracked this outlaw right into Bannock. Followed him easy by the shoes on his horse. The blacksmith's stamp showed real clear in the dust." Sheriff Buffum turned a little and looked up at Troy with a whimsical, wry smile.

"Well, sir; we figured we'd just catch him by stopping every rider coming out of town north, and south too. I had the south end of town, the government men had the north road." The cigarette went underfoot and was deftly decapitated with a small, blunt spur rower. "We never found anyone packing any bullion at all, and that's funny, too, isn't it?"

"Yeah, I guess so," Troy said, angry at himself because the roof of his mouth was dry as alkali. "Still— you didn't know for sure he came here, did you?"

Tom nodded solemnly. "Yeah. 'Course, he might've ridden out of town before we blocked the roads. Only I don't think so."

"Well, what do you think happened to him? He rode east or west maybe, across the range, without using the road?"

"Nope. I doubt that. We'd have noticed him leaving town that way, Troy." Tom was silent for a moment, looking languidly out the big front opening of the forge, watching traffic go by outside, then he shrugged. "Hell—it could be several things. Maybe he hid the silver hereabouts, in town I mean. Maybe he didn't bring any with him after all, although I'm sure he did.

10

There wasn't any cash in the loot. Maybe something else, Troy, like concealing it some darned way and riding past the government men."

"You have something in mind?"

Tom arose, stretched slightly, flexing his long, thin arms and sinewy shoulders, shaking his head as he did so. "No; not especially. Nothing but ideas—and they aren't worth a damn until you can prove 'em." He smiled again in the raffish, deferential way he had, let his arms fall back to his sides and shrugged elaborately. "Well—that's given you an idea that a lawman's work's got sweat in it, too, eh?"

"I reckon," Troy said trying to match the smile, having small success and being smart enough not to force it until it was an obvious, glaring failure to the sheriff. "Who you reckon this outlaw was, Tom?"

Buffum's eyes held Troy's glance with its intensity. "I know who he was. Jeb Carter. Old Jeb the horsebreaker. You recollect him don't you?"

"Yeah." Troy sensed that Tom knew more than he was saying, finally. It scared him a little, but made him suddenly antagonistic in a defensive way, too. That was the new Troy Muller. "Sure; I reckon we all do. You and me and Cynthia—and Ellie."

"Sure we do," Tom said. "Ellie and me were talking about him the other night. The same day I talked to you about him." Buffum seemed to study his next words carefully, then he threw Troy another smile, slightly different though, and started for the door.

"Troy—when you rake the shop floor out, you ought to rake the back alley a little way too. It gets kind of cluttered up, what with parings and all—and shoeprints."

Troy didn't answer. He stood there hearing the

11

hubbub of the forge, watching the lean, lithe form of the sheriff go across the shop and out into the dazzling sunlight beyond where the traffic of Bannock swirled by, jerking dust devils alive in the powdery fine, brown pavement of dirt that filled the roadway all summer long. His heart was pounding with a lurching indecision. Tom Buffum knew! If not about the shoes themselves, at least that Jeb had been to Muller's Forge, and he had guessed pretty shrewdly at that, what might have happened to that silver bar—what actually had happened, in fact.

Troy went back to work again with his eyes slitted more than usual and his mouth a bloodless streak sucked back against his teeth. He wasn't very good company for a few days after that. Only at home with Cynthia. The change was emerging, too. He was less talkative, more inclined to look off over people's heads, and worked with something automatic operating his big body, leaving his mind free.

Perhaps it was the very preoccupation that caused the accident. Certainly it contributed, but he wasn't watching when Sweeney's private stud lashed out, caught him along the side and lay him, gasping, ten feet away.

Cin waited on him with tenderness for a few days, but he could see the suspicion and dislike forming in her that well people have for those who are sick too long.

He lay in the bed and thought of the torn muscles in his back and the broken ribs. The bones would heal, but a blacksmith's back was his stock in trade. Once hurt, it never stood him again without agony. That was one of the things all blacksmiths understood. Troy stared out the window. Now what? He could sell the shop, it was a prosperous business. After that—what? How would he

12

be able to hold her now? He only had this one trade, and it was something he couldn't return to, the doctor had told him that plainly enough. Still, he had to get the money to buy a horse for the yellow wheeled buggy—for Cin. How?

Six days after the accident he was sitting on the porch of their home, smoking a cigar thoughtfully, hearing the sounds of the summer night around him, as well as Cin's small, musical noises inside the house where she did the supper dishes.

It was a beautiful night with the tattered, purple tapestry of the sky letting light shine through the millions of holes that were stars. A fragrant night, with moon wash sage and pine and junipers scenting it. Over it all was the sound of Bannock, too, his town. Men whooping to one another, laughing and making the nickelodeon in the Palace Bar, Bannock's best and largest, send splashes of thin, wavering music out into the stillness.

Troy was absorbing the smells and sounds and didn't see the sharp edged shadow that came down the side of his house to the accompaniment of dogs barking close by, until the man spoke.

"Troy—don't look around. Go on smoking your cigar."

He started in the chair in spite of himself. It was the same soft, clear voice he'd heard the day he'd made the silver horseshoes, and he obeyed it, more startled than anything else, letting his brooding thoughts fall away.

"Listen—that was a good job. I owe you an explanation."

"You owe me nothing, like I told you then."

"Well, I'll tell you anyway. I saw Tom Buffum set up his roadblock. He took the south end of town. I couldn't

hide the damned bar, so I had the shoes made. It got me past the law like that." Carter snapped his fingers sharply. "Saved my neck, I'll tell you."

"Tom knew you were at the shop. He drifted in later and told me, in a round about way, that is."

"The hell." Carter hunkered in the deep shadows beside the porch. "Tom's smart. Always was a sly sort of hombre, with that smile and easy going way of his. I reckon lots of outlaws have sold him short and been caught up over it."

There was a moment of silence when the raucousness of the Palace drifted down to them, muted. It seemed to rouse the bandit from his reverie. He squirmed, twisting so that he could see Troy's face.

"I got a proposition for you, Troy."

"No thanks." It was said as drily as a Fall wind blowing through corn husks.

Carter chuckled softly. Surprisingly, it was a musical, altogether pleasant, appealing sound.

"Wait a minute, compadre. Don't be so jumpy. Troy—I got a lot of money. Not just that silver bullion, but a lot besides. The bullion's cash now anyway. Now here—I want to invest it, you see. I want to own the Palace Bar. Naturally, I can't just sashay up to old man Julian and make an offer, so I want you to do it."

"Me? Buy the Palace for you?"

Jeb wagged his head. Troy turned a little and shot him a glance. All he could see clearly was the eyes, bright and wide and never still, in the bewhiskered face.

"No. You buy the place for you. In other words, I'll give you the money and you buy the Palace for yourself. Between you and me, we'll know I own it, you see, but no one else will."

"I don't exactly understand, Jeb."

"All right," there was a sound of importance in the clipped, clear words. "Someday I'll quit, Troy. When I do, I want a legitimate business to fall back on. The Palace will be it. Now you understand?" Troy didn't answer and the cigar in his mouth was cold, dead. He was staring obliquely up the road toward the lighted saloon. He heard Carter speak again as he watched the men come and go through the swinging doors.

"Half and half, Troy. No investment on your part, except loyalty to me. You run the place, take half the profit, bank the other half for me. That's simple enough, isn't it?"

Troy was nodding with a light in his dark eyes. "Simple enough, I reckon." Here was the solution to his problem of a ruined back—and keeping Cin. He clamped down hard on the cigar, bit through it in fact, and let the acid juice sour the lining of his mout.

"This money we're going to buy the place with. Is it stolen money?" There was no immediate answer. Troy gestured with one hand. "I mean—can it be traced to a robbery, Jeb?"

"Oh—no. It's from a legitimate bank. No; that part of the thing's safe enough."

"Well, what isn't safe, then?"

"Nothing. Not a damned thing so long as you play square with me and keep your mouth shut. Do you like it, Troy?"

He didn't have to think about it. He already had. Just one thing mattered to him anyway, and once more, Jeb Carter was providing the means for keeping it close to him.

"Yeah. Where is this money? How much you reckon it'll take to make Julian sell?"

The shadow moved slightly. A heavy, round leather

bag fell on to the porch beside Troy's feet. The answer came after. "I got no idea about those questions. There's enough there to buy the damned town. All I'm saying is, get the Palace, and get it in your name. Money's left over, use it on stock and such. I don't know anything about business, Troy: you do. That's why I came to you." The shadow arose abruptly and moved close to the porch. Troy turned then, looked down into the thin, cold features and saw an ungloved hand extended.

"I reckon this'll be binding enough, between us, Troy. Don't you?"

Troy leaned over slightly, ignored the stabs of quick, earnest pain in his back, and grasped the hand, not smiling.

"I reckon," he said.

And that was all there was to it. Troy Muller and Jeb Carter were partners. It took three days of negotiating with old man Julian, but the Palace Bar passed to Troy, and with it came a surge of prominence and respect he'd never known existed. With Cin, too, there was this new look of regard.

"Troy—all these years? From the shop, honey?"

He smiled and nodded to his lie. His regard for her had changed to something perilously close to contempt that she, who was always so smart, had been outsmarted by his falseness.

"Hell yes; you think I wanted to be a smith all my life?"

The level gray eyes glowed with open admiration. She crossed the little parlor and stood in front of his chair, seeing again the might and massiveness of him, and feeling some of the breathlessness she had once felt before, when he had come courting her.

"I wondered, Troy. I wondered lots of times." She

16

made a small motion with her head that was an indication of dead doubts. "The other men went ahead, some of them. It used to make me sick, seeing you still a blacksmith."

His dark eyes were ironic behind the small smile he wore. "Blacksmithing isn't good enough for you, Cin?"

"Of course, dear. It's just that I used to think you were too smart to be one forever."

"And now? What are you thinking now?"

"That I know you're too smart to make shoes. But—there was a lot of doubt, for a while, Troy."

He almost mocked her, but his weakness held him back. Instead, he patted his lap with one hand. "Been a long time since you sat on my lap, girl. Sit down."

She did, with deliberate grace and candor, while her mind soared to the new heights she dared to dream of, when her husband owned the richest, most successful saloon in Bannock. The yellow wheeled buggy was only a starter.

CHAPTER TWO

TROY WATCHED THE WEALTH IN THE DUAL BANK accounts grow. He had more than prestige now, he had money too, and it influenced him more than the homage. His dark eyes grew narrower, more veiled and watchful. His great body grew soft too, until the last of the tawny muscles were sheathed in a covering of white fat. It didn't destroy his power or strength any, it just lessened the endurance, but Troy Muller was past having to endure hardship and labor again.

He stood at the far end of the bar, not ten feet from his office door, when Tom Buffum came in, nodded to the bartenders, several lounging, mid-day stragglers, and went down the line until he stood at the front of the bar, across from Troy. The whimsical, sardonic eyes appraised the larger man.

"Troy; you're getting soft."

The dark eyes were nettled for just a second, then the huge shoulders rose and fell. "I reckon. Likely to in a place like this, Tom. How's lawing?"

Buffum shrugged too, ordered a beer and waited for it before he answered. "Oh; so so. Still got a few headaches in it, like always. Wish I could shed 'em like you shed that job of yours. The one with all the sweat in it."

Troy instantly recalled the day and circumstances when he'd made that remark. The dark eyes held to Tom's face. "You will one of these days, Tom. How's Ellie?"

Buffum drained his beer and set the glass down without answering. His eyes raised to a great horned owl, perched on a small limb over the backbar mirror, poised in perpetual flight, its tiny, malevolent glass eyes fixed roundly on a distant Eternity.

"I said how's Ellie?"

"I heard you. She's about like always. We were talking about you buying the Palace, last night at dinner."

"Yeah?" Troy couldn't shake the uneasiness Buffum's manner inspired in him. He liked the sheriff and had, since they were boys together, but he didn't underestimate him at all. Not after that day in the forge.

"Yeah. Ellie said you were changing. I said I didn't think a man ever changed. Some just had stuff inside 'em that didn't come out until they got in a pinch of some kind."

Troy rapped the bar softly with his knuckles, eyeing the sheriff. His thoughts weren't bitter, but they weren't pleasant either. He remembered Ellie Buffum too well. She had always stirred him deeply. Had, in fact, right up to the day he'd met Cynthia and in a wild, passionate moment, married her. Ellie still stirred him, even in memory. The softness of her violet eyes, the way her nose turned up a little and had a saddle of freckles across it. The way she held her full underlip between her teeth and frowned when she was thinking. He turned abruptly and walked to his office door, went in and shoved the panel closed behind himself, without saying another word to Tom.

The sheriff watched his retreat with a thoughtful glance, opening and closing his left fist around the cool, moist beer glass.

Troy sat before the desk and let his thoughts run a gamut inside his head. He had achieved the success necessary to keep Cin. It was something else now, as well. It was money and power—and a certain ruthlessness that was a natural offshoot of both. Cin was a trinket now, and that thought surprised him more than anything else. He had never thought, or imagined in his most unhappy hours, that he would ever regard her as anything but the breath to his existence; actually, he loved her as much as before. Now, though, she was less often in his mind.

Someone knocked on the office door. Troy growled permission to enter. It was a man named Campbell. Loring Campbell of the Keystone Stage & Transfer Company. Owner of the line that had the mail and bullion contract between Bannock and Herd's Crossing, the next town up country, twenty-three miles north. Troy flagged one great arm at a chair.

19

"What brought you out, Loring?" There was no friendliness in the tone or words. Just a blunt question by a man learning to dispense with courtesy.

"Troy—would you be interested in part ownership in my business?" Campbell's watery eyes were slightly protruding, wholly without tenderness and carefully veiled over with the steel varnish of inner hardness. Dedication to a dollar. Troy's look had the same sheen.

"What brought that up?"

Campbell fished for a cigar in his coat. "Too many losses. Government's going to cancel my contract for bullion, I think."

Troy smiled. "Well—you're honest about it anyway. How do you know this is going to happen?"

"Friend of mine in Santa Fe wrote me about it couple days ago."

"What else?"

"What do you mean?"

Troy snorted. "You didn't come in here to peddle me an interest in that line of your's, then tell me why you want money, so honest and all—unless you've got other troubles as well. What's it all about, Loring?"

Campbell chewed his cigar with a speculative, rhythmic motion, appraising the hard face across the room from him. "I'd—rather not say."

Troy threw up his hands. "Hell's fire! My money don't go out that easy, Loring. I might buy in at that. But not without knowing everything about the business there is to know. You want to keep secrets. Loring— then keep the line too."

Campbell squirmed, chewed a little faster and let his glance sweep overhead, then back to Troy Muller's face. "You'd get madder'n hell, Troy. But—I need the money."

20

"All right, dammit; spit it out."

"These robberies—folks say you got a hand in 'em."

The shock was stunning. Troy sat like a statue, glaring at Campbell. Seeing the man's color fade before his glance, but scarcely noticing. Instantly, something Jeb Carter had once said came to his mind. 'Funny how the word gets around'. He felt the old tightening in his stomach, wondering whether guesswork or observation, or maybe Jeb himself, had steered this suspicion to him. Anger came up out of him and washed his mind in waves that made the temple in the side of his head throb. Then Campbell was talking again.

". . . believe it, of course. But, well, I figure it this way. When a man gets a name he might as well have the game too. Maybe these road agents'll hear you're in the business with me. They'd slack off, Troy. Leave our stages alone—maybe—then I could finish out the year with no more bullion robberies. A line loses three times and the contract's canceled. I've lost twice now. Your money and prestige'd salvage things—I feel."

Troy's tongue came down off the roof of his mouth slowly. Stiff and unnatural like a rough piece of wood soaked in brine. "Where'd this talk start?"

"God knows, Troy; I don't."

The big hands went forward on the desk, clasped, with white knuckles showing how they gripped one another. Troy's dark eyes were savage and intent. "Listen to me, Campbell; I'll buy into your damned stage line on one condition."

"Yes?"

"Tell me where you heard this talk—and don't lie, damn you, or you can starve!"

Loring Campbell's cigar began its even rise and fall again. His weak eyes arose and held to Troy's face

21

while he figured chances. There was little alternative. He needed Muller's money—and badly.

"All right; all right. It's common enough talk, Troy. I expect everyone knows about it except you, anyway. I heard it from Colt Albert."

Troy regarded the older man with such scorn that his fact was tinctured by it. "That damned fool."

"Sure," Campbell said defensively. "I know. That's the point; if Colt knows about it, so does everyone else. You see?"

Troy saw just one thing. He'd have to talk to Jeb Carter, which wasn't easy to do because Jeb never told him where he could be reached. He'd just materialize out of the evening, when he was around Bannock, and that was all. He looked over at Campbell again, disdainfully.

"How much you need?"

"Five-thousand."

The big, shaggy head went up and down, once. "All right. Meet me here tomorrow at ten. I'll have the papers and the money."

Campbell's gratitude, sincere or not, was cut short, and he left the office. Troy didn't move for ten minutes after the caller had gone. He sat like a man in a trance, then he arose restlessly, went out into the saloon where one look at his bleak, forbidding face forestalled greetings by the gathering customers, and went outside, turned north towards Mrs. Murphy's boarding house, where the Mullers had the entire top floor, and strode in preoccupied movement until he was home, upstairs, and saw Cin taking off her gloves by a massively, ornately, framed mirror, examining her face with obvious satisfaction.

She turned at his entrance, mildly surprised at seeing

him home early. He appraised her figure, saw the small signals of maturity showing where rich living and food were making their soft paddings.

"You're awfully early, Troy." There was a hint of irritation in the words. He looked at her sharply, wondering if he hadn't heard uneasiness there too.

"Does it make any difference, Cin?"

She shrugged, avoiding his glance and finishing with the gloves. "No, except that I just got in myself and haven't started supper yet." She tossed the gloves on a table and threw him a cool smile. "I'll get your beer."

He was still standing there, musing, when she returned. Unconsciously he took the beer, grunted thanks and drained the glass. A little trickled past his lips and caught annoyingly on his stony chin. He set the glass down, swore under his breath, searched for a handkerchief that wasn't there, saw Cin's gloves lying there, took one up and dabbed at the beer. The strong, pungent aroma of a cigar struck him forcibly. Lowering the glove he regarded it with astonishment, sniffed again, put it down slowly and strode unevenly toward a window that looked out over Bannock.

So that's what makes them that way. He'd known faithless women in his lifetime—from a distance—and had wondered casually why they were like that. The answer had come to him as he crossed to the window. Husbands that indulged them. Sold their souls as he had done, to keep them. Grown like granite to give them more—and leisure—which they used to flirt. Lacking moral standards, they went farther when they felt like it. Not for love, he knew, because Cynthia wasn't really capable of love. And that too, came naturally to his mind. It cut him hard under the heart when he confirmed it by recollections over the years. Coldness, aloofness at time, selfishness. He jammed huge fists into his pockets and clenched them against the certain knowledge that something like a cherished dream inside him was lying in shattered ruins around his feet.

Cynthia came into the room, gave him a long, level glance, and smiled with that old look that could mean everything—or nothing. He couldn't force a false smile back, so just turned stolidly on thick legs and regarded her, feeling the knife in his heart twist until he would have enjoyed being alone—and far away—so he could have cried out.

"Troy—would there be some way you could use a young man at the Palace? I mean—he's not a bartender, or anything, but—"She let it die there, looking into his face for help that wasn't there. Only a dawning suspicion. A reluctant, dragging willingness to look at her. Even small resentment that he didn't hate her—couldn't hate her, in spite of the vast blow to him that had come too easily, so unsuspectingly and suddenly.

"What's his name?" There was the sound of lead falling against hard earth the way he said it, but she didn't notice.

"Will Jennings. He's from over at Herd's Crossing. Comes from good family."

"Well," he said drily, softly—cuttingly sarcastic. "That makes a difference. Especially to a blacksmith—who owns a saloon."

"Troy!" She saw it then all right. Would have been blind not to see it. The beautiful gray eyes widened. If it was guilt that widened them he couldn't tell.

"Why should I hire him?"

"I asked you to."

"Why did you ask, Cin?"

She had small splotches of red under her gray eyes

now, letting something show that slumbered beneath the surface. Contempt, maybe, for this great hulking man with the rough embrace and direct methods. The desire to hurt him was plain in her face.

"Because—I thought it might not hurt the Palace any—to have a—a—better class man working there!"

Troy's face twisted a little, the dark eyes glowed somberly at her without blinking. "He must be quality, Cin, to get all this warmth out of you—all right." He nodded at her. "I never could—unless I bought it."

He moved deliberately toward her and didn't stop until less than two feet separated them. His anger kept rising, feeding itself from all the agonizing uncertainties of the long line of yesterdays, and the inner knowledge, no matter how muffled, of what he had done to himself because of her.

"You!" She said it with more breath than the word required, gray eyes shades darker in no long hidden or controlled fury. "Bought it! You—filthy beast."

He saw the hand coming through the air like talons, fingers crooked intentionally, instinctively, in every female animal's posture of offense, and didn't move. The nails tore at his face, slid through the gouges they made.

Strangely, he was smiling, although the taste of his own blood was in his mouth. Smiling while the final formula of chemical change was enacted within him, and the old Troy Muller was vanished forever.

It was like that, that Ellie Buffum saw him striding through the night at the far, south end of Bannock. She stopped when he swung in close, letting the soft night breeze with its hint of later coldness, rustle his string tie, his wavy auburn hair and twist the long ends of his Prince Albert coat.

25

Troy saw her faintly, by outline, but knew her before he was close enough to see her face. He was thankful, instantly, for the shadows that hid the less vivid marks of struggle on his face. Only the long, throbbing scratches showed. He nodded at her.

"Ellie—" He groped, wondered and looked desperately for the rest of it, but there was no more, so he said her name again.

"Ellie."

"Good evening, Troy." She was looking up into his face but nothing more would come out past the sudden lump in her chest. There was a definite bleakness about his ruggedly handsome face that stilled her words.

He smiled and felt the stabs of angry flesh where the scratches were. He thought it was a pleasant smile but to Ellie Buffum it was almost a leer of triumph over some vast secret.

"Ellie—God!—walk with me a ways."

She didn't move. Just looked up at him with doubt and perplexity in her face, then the smallest wrinkle appeared over the saddle of freckles across her small, upturned nose, and she put her head on one side, gathering her underlip between her teeth and regarding him oddly.

"You're—in trouble, aren't you, Troy?"

His smile turned into an abrupt, reckless, ironic laugh. She saw the sparkle in his eyes and bit harder on her lip. There was still a little vestige of the old easy going, quiet Troy Muller there—somewhere—underneath all this other man—this new Troy Muller with his spiraling wealth and whispered reputation as a consort of outlaws.

"Trouble, Ellie? I'm always in it—or just getting out of it. Please—" his voice changed suddenly. The last flame in his heart died out then, squelched by her

26

calmness; her quiet, unafraid, unimpressed appraisal of him. "Just a short walk—Ellie."

They walked south, past the rows of little houses of townsmen, until they came to the less savory tarpaper shacks of less fortunate citizens, then even the plankwalk petered out and they were still moving through the deep scarlet evening, over the trackless rangeland.

"Ellie—I am a fool. A stupid, goddarned fool."

She threw him a dark look. "You can be all those things Troy—without being blasphemous about it."

He grinned in spite of a heart turning heavy within him. at the tart, practical way she said it. "All right; you'll agree with what I mean—if not with the way I say it, then."

She stopped by a gnarled, hoary old oak, stunted and beaten shapeless by the wild winds of spring and fall, and bowed with the snow burdens and heat blastings of years out of mind. He stood before her, towering above her slightness, seeing for the first time, as she was and always had been. Small, self-contained, eminently practical, and with a background of the patient old oak that was like her eternal spirit. It startled him that such thoughts, so nearly poetic, were in his head.

"What have you done, Troy? Do—you want to tell me?"

He didn't reply right away. Just stood there gazing at her in surprise, still in the grip of the strange thoughts that had been in his mind so fleetingly. Then he looked down, saw the new spring grass and motioned toward it in half embarrassment.

"Sit down, Ellie." He dropped down beside her, catching a little of her fragrance when a small, chilly zephyr blew around them.

"There's damned little to tell. I—married the wrong woman for one thing. I've—sold myself out, for another."

Ellie's dark eyes were soft, unblinking. "Troy—you made a bargain—with Cynthia."

He nodded. "Sure; I've made bad bargains before. You can buy your way out—or something—usually."

"But—you don't want to, Troy. Not from her."

He looked up, surprised. "Don't I?"

"No." She shook her head slightly at him. "Because you still love her."

He didn't answer. The stars were like flickering icicles wind-whipped into marbles, overhead. There was a definite coolness in the air. It wasn't cold yet, but the promise of cold coming was in their breath.

"I—don't know, Ellie. God knows—I don't."

"A woman knows, though, Troy. It's in your face. In your eyes. Is that the trouble you're in?"

"Part of it. There's—another thing. Talk. Rumors. I heard today folks're saying I'm in with outlaws."

"I heard that long ago, Troy. Just after you bought the Palace."

His big head came up quickly. There was a vicious light in the dark eyes. "You too, Ellie? You believe it?"

"I didn't say I believed it. Just that I'd heard it."

"But—where in tarnation would a thing like that start?"

She looked away from him for a second, letting her eyes wander back toward the rich, golden shafts of lamplight that were blossoming out, back in town, then she looked around resolutely again.

"Troy—you're so—awfully blind."

"What do you mean?" He had lost some of the urgency from his voice. It was being brought into him

28

tenderly and forcibly that Cin hadn't been his sole mistake with a woman. The old, deep stirring for Ellie was coming to life like it had never been dead before. With all its old ardor and anguish. He looked at her face and felt his heart lurch heavily, miss a long beat, then rocket again in the dark cavity of his chest.

"What do you mean, Ellie?"

"Troy—you're a big man now. Everyone knows you—whether they respect or like you, or not. Anyway—they won't say things about you, where you'll be likely to hear them."

"So?"

"So; Troy—you are alone. And—being alone, you have to develop an ability to see and hear what folks won't tell or show you. Do you understand?"

"Well; in a way—I reckon. But what's that got to do with this talk?"

"I said you were blind. You are. After you bought the Palace, there were men in town who knew Jeb Carter. Outlaws perhaps; I don't know. But I do know that they said you bought the place in partnership with Jeb."

His mind was raging in an instant. So it had been Jeb after all. Cold eyed, reckless, heartless Jeb Carter. He hadn't ever thought——. He shrugged.

"Damn it all. Ellie—can't a man trust *anyone*?"

"Of course, Troy. Only some men are blind. They don't know the difference in the kinds of men they can trust. You don't, for instance. Jeb is a renegade. He always will be. It's in his heart, Troy. A man like that could never be trusted—at all."

He straightened in shock, looking at her. "Does Tom know about this?"

"You're the only one that knows for certain, Troy. The rest of us have heard rumors, is all. Tom has heard

29

them, naturally."

Troy groaned and let his big shoulders slump. Ellie put a hand out instinctively and held his arm in her fingers. He turned with bitterness etched in his face for the second time that day, and smiled at her.

"Well—Ellie; it's lucky you never married me after all—isn't it?"

Just how it happened, he never was clear in his mind later. Only that she made a low, gentle sob and was in his arms and he was kissing her. letting gentleness keep their mouths together. And the rust color mounted into his face, which was hidden by the night, for which he was once more thankful, and her fingers were pressing his face down and running through the thick auburn hair.

"Ellie!"

She didn't speak, knowing as women do intuitively, the language of love is silence.

"Good—Lord—Ellie!"

His shock was so apparent that it struck a chord of humor in her. She smiled a little wanly, looking at him. "Was it that bad, Troy?"

"Oh Ellie—it isn't right—this way—now."

"No," she agreed gravely, "but I'm not sorry."

He looked at her for a long time saying nothing, then raised his arms, holding them outward and open. She went into them again. That time he could feel the moistness of her cheeks against his. and the fire in them as well when he covered her mouth with his.

Ellie pushed against his big chest gently, firmly, and he let her go, holding her shoulders and staring down into her eyes.

"I'm sorry this happened, Ellie. I've got enough trouble for one man. Now you've got a share of it too. It isn't fair to you."

30

She wagged her head in a small gesture, holding his glance,with her own. "It hasn't occurred to you that I might be willing to share it, willingly, has it?"

He made an inarticulate sound deep in his throat. "It isn't your trouble, honey; it's mine. I don't want you to be hurt or smeared by it."

She shook free of his hands and pushed herself slowly away from him, warmth and tenderness and undestanding radiating from her.

"Well—I want to share it, Troy." She watched him come closer, stand towering above her, very solemn faced. "Is—it true, about you and Jeb Carter?"

He nodded, letting the silence lend an emphasis that carried the full import to her, without any alibis.

Her eyes wavered; there was a hint of bitterness in them. "You have changed, Troy. You have. I'm sorry."

"It makes a whale of a difference—doesn't it?"

She made a wry smile and shook her head at him. "Well—only in you. Not in me."

Troy made a slight, slashing movement with one hand. "Ellie, I love you and always have. Even—after I married Cin. It's—a devil of a thing to say, but I have—always."

She took his arm in both hands and squeezed it until he was conscious of the pain from her fingernails. "All right; you're being honest with me. I'll be honest with you. I've never stopped loving you, Troy Muller—and never will. Now," she released his arm and moved away from him, back toward town before the tortured look in his eyes made her weak again. "Let's go back."

They did. Walking slowly and close, so that their arms touched, sending spirals of exquisite agony through both of them. And in silence, until they were outside the sheriff's little house, where Ellie kept her bachelor brother's

31

domicile. There they stopped, turned instinctively and regarded one another. The night was a dull black blanket pulled up close around the neck of the land.

Ellie's voice was soft, like thistles blowing against a wall. "Kiss me again, Troy."

He bent down reverently without touching her. Their lips met gently, just a small, gentle brush of lips upon lips that increased the ache within them, then he straightened and smiled at her.

"I love you Ellie—so very, very much."

Then he was gone, striding back down toward his Palace bar, a big, rich man, erect, massive and indomitable. Ellie watched him until the darkness left her only memories and the softly muted sounds of his footfalls, then she turned, went through the picket gate, up the duckboards toward the porch, head down, and blind to everything, but not dead, so she heard the sound of a chair squeaking on the porch, raised her eyes in horror and saw Tom's profile dark against the lighter darkness of the night, and heard his voice reach out to her. "Ellie!"

CHAPTER THREE

WHEN TROY ENTERED THE PALACE THE NOISE STRUCK him like something off-key and violent. It slammed up against his memories of Ellie under the oak tree and jarred his thoughts with its raucousness. For the first time, the knowledge that this was now his life—this bedlam, smell of green liquor and spit encrusted sawdust underfoot, old tobacco and sweat, human and horse—was borne in solidly upon him.

He crossed through the mob of men, towering above

32

them, feeling their closeness and smiling mechanically into their shiny eyes, like rum soaked olives, glistening moist and stupid looking, and got to the door of his office before anyone hailed him. He turned, waved generously, made up a forced smile that was a distinct failure, twisted the office door and entered, closed the door, raised his eyes and froze against the panel.

"Had me worried, Troy. Thought you might not come back tonight."

"Howdy, Jeb."

The outlaw's cold eyes flashed in surprise over the scratches on his face but, like Ellie, who also recognized them for what they were, he said nothing.

A bottle of rye whiskey was on a table beside the renegade. The sticky little glass beside it showed that Jeb Carter knew how to kill time.

Troy crossed the room on heavy legs, dropped into his chair, reached for the liquor glass and downed one before he regarded his partner again.

"How's business, Troy?"

"Good. Like always, we're making money." He fished out deposit slips and tossed them across to Carter. Watched the gunman glance hurriedly at the bottom balances, smile icily and toss them back on to the table.

"Better'n stealing money—almost."

Troy shrugged. "Isn't much difference, Jeb. Your way or my way."

"I reckon not. Only that there's risk my way."

Troy leaned forward, feeling his Prince Albert draw tight over his upper arms and shoulders. He stared at Carter's cruel, hard features, and frowned a little. "When you going to retire?"

The outlaw was startled and showed it. "Why?" You're doing fine alone, aren't you?"

"Yeah; in a way. As far as the Palace is concerned—anyway."

"Oh," Carter said softly. "You got troubles on the side—that it?"

"I've got 'em all right, Jeb, but they've got nothing to do with the Palace—or you."

Carter mused thoughtfully, regarding Troy levelly. "Listen—Troy. Money'll make trouble for men, if they don't know how to live with it. It can change a man like nothing else can." He laughed bitterly. "Look at me, if you want an example. As a bronc-buster I made better'n any straight rider. It wasn't enough though, so I took a flier at robbing a stage, got recognized—and now here I am. Money—hell—I got it. More'n I can ever spend. What's it done for me? This! I figured someday I'd be able to quit, settle down—and all. I was kidding myself, Troy. I can't ever quit, and finally I know it, too." He smiled for the first time without making it a levered up, forced grimace. It reminded Troy of the old Jeb Carter, the horse-breaker: reckless, laughing, wild and unpredictable. Except that this smile had wistfulness in it.

"And now you want to get out and give it all back to me. That right, Troy?"

"I reckon." Troy pushed back in the chair, leaned far back and regarded his partner stoically. "Yeah; I—made a bargain, Jeb. I'm not quitting—but I'd sure like to wiggle out, someway."

Carter shook his head back and forth slowly. "There's no way out for you, any more than there is for me, Troy. I can't find another man I'd trust, and I can't run the saloon myself—so that leaves you."

There wasn't any rancor in the outlaw's voice at all. Just a grim finality that made Troy conscious of what

34

Jeb had said before. Money ruins men. Those beyond the law can't ever get completely clear of the degradation that raised them up by lawlessness. He sighed, fished around for a tobacco sack, twisted a cigarette savagely into existence, lit it, inhaled and exhaled gently, into the silence of the office, with its overtone of bedlam from the saloon proper.

"Why you want out, Troy?"

"A lot of things."

"Your wife—maybe?" Carter's eyes were as steady and unmoving as ice.

"That's part of it all right. Another thing, Jeb. I'm buying into the local stage outfit. Half interest. You know how come I'm doing this? Campbell, hombre who owns the lines, came in here today offering to sell me half interest because he'd heard I was in with outlaws and he figured no one would rob his stages if they knew I was a part owner."

Carter slumped a little in his chair. For once, his eyes wavered, slid off Troy's face, raked over the inartistic arrangement of flyspecks on a backwall, then came back again.

"That's my fault, Troy. I'm sorry." He shrugged. "That don't help and I know it. I got glowed up with some of the boys in a back-country rendezvous. Got loud and bragging about my lawful connections."

"You told 'em about me?"

"Yeah. It—was a hell of a thing to do. Like I said, I'm sorry."

"I reckon you are," Troy said drily. "Well—it's done, Jeb."

"All right. You buy into that stage line. I'll pass the word—no one'll bother it." Carter poured himself another shot, downed it, pulled his bearded lips back over his teeth in a savage face, then coughed. "How many holdups they had so far this year?"

"Two. One more'll lose 'em the franchise."

"All right. You got my word for it, boy. No more robberies. Does that make you feel better? about staying on at the Palace, here?"

Troy didn't answer right away. He slumped back in his chair thinking of the rumors, of Ellie under the oaks and the kind of respectability he'd have to have before she'd ever consent to marry him, and of Cynthia—and what it would take to extricate himself there, as well. Money and lots of it would assuage his wife. He knew that very well. So well, in fact, that his intuition told him no stage line on earth would ever pay him enough—but the Palace would. He nodded unhappily.

"All right; I'll stay for a while, Jeb. But you start looking around. Until the end of the year, anyway."

Jeb Carter sighed audibly, letting weariness show in his violent eyes, narrowed now in thought. "There is one feller—but darnit—I don't know, Troy. Hombre named Will Jennings from over by Herd's Crossing. He might do. Hard to say."

Troy's face went wooden, stony hard and lifeless. "Will Jennings? Who is he, Jeb?"

"Oh—manages the Herd's Crossing end of Keystone Stage Line. Young feller, hell with the ladies. Lots of black curly hair and big blue eyes; you know the kind. Seems honest—but a man can't never tell. Trusting people's dangerous business—sometimes, Troy."

"Yeah." The word was dour. He was thinking of what Ellie had said on the same subject and studied Jeb in a new light. "Yeah; sure is—well—I'll be getting along home. You have anything else on your mind?"

"No," Jeb said very slowly. "Just—that—dammit; I

36

don't know, Troy—just don't know." The outlaw arose slowly, tiredly, shaking his head in bewilderment, feeling the pangs of resentment against life and everything in it, which were becoming more and more recurrent in his thinking, then he shrugged, regarded the whiskey bottle with a calculated stare, took it up and dropped it into the pocket of his shapeless coat and walked toward the rear window, turning back just once and fixing Troy with his hot, hard eyes. "I got to think things out for a few days. I'll be back next week—some time. Adios."

"Adios."

Troy sat relaxed and brooding long after Carter had disappeared into the somber gloom outside then he heaved his big frame erect, shook himself like a dog after crossing a creek, and stalked out of the office, back through the press of noisy humanity, cowboys, freighters with their perpetual scorch from the blistering hot land they traversed, townmen in quieter, more. subdued groups, and hangers-on. He turned several times and listened to small talk, jokes and greetings, then he was out past the louvered doors that swung too quietly on their oiled spindles, and the night cold struck his face and made a pleasant, healthful contrast to the rancid, stale odors of the Palace.

Mrs. Murphy's boarding house had lights downstairs, but none on the top floor, where the Muller apartment was. He went into the house, smelled the cabbage odors downstairs, hiked somberly up the steps, unlocked the door and went in, felt for the lamp, lit it, replaced the mantle and felt the chill in the rooms that presaged emptiness—loneliness. He wasn't hungry, so missing dinner didn't bother him at all, but he built a fire in the wood stove before he took off his coat and dropped into a horsehair stuffed, leather rocker—the first one to come to Bannock; Cynthia's pride—and let his head rock back.

Maybe Cynthia had left him. His lips twisted up into a hard smile. Well, if he had to lose her someday, maybe it was better this way. He closed his eyes and wondered about this Will Jennings she had been with—knew. The gargoyle smile persisted. Jennings was being fooled too. He knew it as surely as he knew he was sitting there relaxed. Maybe there had been other fools too, since his interests at the Palace had kept him busy. Fooled by her apparent fire and sturdy build that ironically, definitely—didn't mean any such thing in Cynthia. Even her nickname—Cin—and the way it was pronounced, aided the illusion. Troy laughed suddenly, hugging his secret for comfort, grimly, and letting his mind tiptoe over the cut-glass memories that were sharp and waiting for him to get hurt by them, in the darkness of his brain.

He opened his eyes finally, and looked at the ceiling. Strangely, he had no more than a sense of loss for a convenience. Like a man would lose a saddle, his spurs or his gun, and that astonished him, because he had been so sure, right up to the moment he entered the house, that Cin's loss would be unbearable.

Cautiously, he turned the thing over in his mind and came up with an alarming fact. It hadn't been Cin, after all. Instead it was his inherent fear of being alone; not feeling wanted; not having someone to sweat for and feel that he belonged to.

He reached for his tobacco sack, slowly made a cigarette, lit it and smoked with a faint scowl. Maybe it was because, having been an orphan, alone most of his life, that he held to his fanatical attachment so stubbornly. He shook his head, swore to himself, and fitted in a piece of the thing just as a soft knock came on the outer door. He had lost Cin more than likely. Unconsciously, or perhaps sub-consciously, he was even turning to Ellie as his wife had left the house. Finding his place with the sheriff's sister and losing himself again where he felt he was wanted—needed.

He arose, crossed the room and flung open the door. Tom Buffum stood there, looking up into Troy's face and seeing the snarled skein of thoughts reflected there.

"Come in, Tom. Have a chair."

The sheriff let his hat fall beside the chair he eased down into, moved his holstered gun so it wouldn't gouge the upholstery, and settled back.

"You alone, Troy?"

"Yeah." The dark eyes flickered over Tom's face, read something in the depths, and waited.

"Good. We got a little time then."

"All the time in the world—I think."

Tom looked at him strangely but didn't put the glance into words. He shrugged, looked down at his hands and cleared his throat.

"Funny goddamned life, isn't it?"

"Yeah. Funny as a kick in the groin by an Army mule. What do you mean—particularly?" Troy thought he knew what was coming, but he wasn't prepared for what the sheriff said at all.

"Well—I mean it's funny about you and Jeb Carter. Such opposites in so many things."

The dark eyes narrowed, grew longer and hooded. A wave of something close to sickness swept over Troy. Ellie had told her brother. She must have. He recalled with consummate bitterness what she had said about people being blind. About trusting other people. Even Carter's comments on the same subject came back to him. He bobbed his head up and down slowly, almost in defeat.

"All right, Tom. Say it. All of it."

Buffum's glance came up. There was unhappiness in his whimsical face. "Well—I'll start earlier, Troy. I was sitting on the porch when you and Ellie came back from your walk. Just sort of lazing there—and smoking."

Troy's mind went back vividly to the last kiss. A little of the illness pushed back. Maybe she'd had no alternative, after Tom had seen him kiss her. It was woefully weak and he knew it, but he was grasping at anything now, to keep away from the loneliness again.

"You—saw—what?"

"I saw you kiss her, Troy."

"I see. That's—bad. I—can't say I'm sorry, Tom, because I'm not."

"Well; that's not what I came here about anyway. It's—just—that—well—I don't think you did the fair thing by a damned sight. Also, I think you know it, too." He made a motion with his left hand to forestall the words he saw forming on Troy's lips. "But, that's all personal stuff. We'll work that out between us—someday."

Troy was watching him closer now, feeling the old uneasiness return, that Sheriff Buffum always inspired in him. "What's the other thing, then?"

"Like I said. You and Jeb Carter."

"Where did you hear it?"

"I didn't hear a damned thing I paid any heed to, Troy. But tonight—after you'd left, after you'd kissed Ellie—I was mad, so I walked uptown to see you. I went down the alley, Troy. You want to guess the rest?"

Relief came over the big man in tidal wave proportions. To the devil with Jeb Carter, and Sheriff Buffum, too. It hadn't been Ellie. She hadn't said anything after all. He actually smiled, and Tom was startled by the sudden happiness in the rugged face.

"Sure; you saw Jeb Carter. Maybe you saw him in the office if you did you should have thrown down on him—that's your job."

"No; I saw him mount up. By the time I'd recognized him, he was riding away, fast."

Troy nodded. "So?"

"Listen Troy, I heard the rumors a long time ago. Right after you bought the Palace. Well—I've known you ever since we were kids. And liked you. Not for Ellie's sake either, because you gave her a raw deal. Anyway—I knew about you two the day you worked up the silver into horseshoes for him."

"How'd you find out about that?"

Tom smiled wryly. "Easy. After the federal marshals left, I took up the trail. Silver's softer'n hell, Troy. I found lots of it on rocks, had it assayed and knew what had happened."

"But you never came back after me?"

Tom shrugged. "No proof, Troy, or I would've. Not good enough evidence. The law gives you every break."

"Maybe," Troy said. "And maybe it's you giving me those breaks."

Tom laughed hollowly. "Don't kid yourself. After what you did to Ellie, even though I liked you, I'd of nailed your damned hide to a cross—if I could've."

"You have enough proof this time, Tom?"

The sheriff shook his head wearily. "Nope. Just evidence that you and Jeb are friends. 'Course, I could nail you for not arresting him when he was in your place, but that's not too good either."

"Why not?"

"Because, all you'd swear to is that you didn't know

41

he was Jeb Carter."

Troy nodded curtly. "That's right."

"Anyway—that's not what I'm here about. I'm going to ask you a couple of questions, Troy, because I'm in one hell of a spot."

"Shoot."

Tom's glance was speculative. "Truthful answers, Troy?"

"As long as I can, Tom. Let's put it this way. If I've got to lie to you, I'll tell you so."

Buffum nodded. "Fair enough. Are you and Jeb in partners at the Palace?"

"Yes."

"Hell! I hated that answer. All right; Troy—are you going to stay with it? Keep up running with this darned gunslinger?"

"That's harder, Tom. I told him I wasn't, tonight."

"Why?"

"A lot of reasons. Ellie's one of 'em, Tom. The others I'll keep to myself."

"Yeah. Now—will you tell me when Jeb's coming back?"

Troy didn't answer for a moment, but his face told tho sheriff all he had to know on that question, long before Troy spoke. "Tom, you know better than to ask me a thing like that."

Buffum arose slowly, stood wide legged before Troy's chair and glowered down at the larger man. "Troy, I'm going to pass a sort of personal law now. One that isn't in the books. Stay away from Ellie!"

The silence grew tangible and solid of core in the room. Troy stood up too, saying nothing, thinking he couldn't obey this order even if he wanted to, then he shook his head.

"I'm sorry, Tom. I thought it might end like this. Us across the fence from one another. Honestly though, I never thought it'd be over Ellie."

"Well, it is. That's more than a warning, Troy. You hurt her bad once. I won't see it done again; you've got my word on it. Don't go near her again—ever!"

When Troy stayed silent, the sheriff turned and walked to the door. "There's no sense in us talking about you and Carter any more, Troy. You made the choice, and now it's your problem, but I'll tell you this, the first chance I get to nail either of you, or both, I'm going to do it." He opened the door, went part way through and looked back again. "I said I liked you— well, I did; still do in spite of what you've done—but from now on, Troy, it's going to be just the law and nothing else."

"Tom." The name sounded flat, forced out under pressure, and colorless. "I'm going down to see Ellie tonight." He saw the muscles in Buffum's face writhe up into tight knots around his jaw. "I'll put it up to her. She's the one to decide, not you or me."

"Like hell. Ellie loves you Troy. You knocked her world down once, but I'll be darned if I'm going to stand by and see you do it again. This time, I'll sit in the game."

Troy reached down for his coat, shrugged into it and turned toward the stove. "Well; do me this favor, anyway. Let's call this visit something outside of your jurisdiction."

"Will it be the last call you'll make on her?"

Troy closed the stove damper down with a savage thrust, feeling the anger welling up into his head like fire. "I won't promise, Tom. Maybe; it'll be up to her."

The sheriff closed the door behind him without

43

another glance or word. His face was pale and set, and his usually calm eyes held a determination that shone clearly in spite of the gloom.

Troy wandered through the rooms, drank a glass of beer and leaned against the kitchen counter thoughtfully. Again, the wonder of all the complexities closed in on him, leaving a sensation of warped tightness to his personal world. He put the glass down, made another cigarette and smoked it until it was small, then went into the cold, ravished bedroom, found the .41 under-and-over derringer, dropped it into his side pocket and left the place almost eagerly, because the warmth from the stove had made it seem more like home, and resurrected memories, unpleasant, but still suffused with his own longings.

Outside, Bannock was a series of sharp edged silhouettes that allowed orange lamplight to trickle from windows, down the sides of houses, across the plankwalk, out over the dusty, manure stained roadway, and lie like weak pools, in the filth.

He walked on the opposite side of the road from the Palace and heard the noise of the nickelodeon, the ragged, untamed voices of the riders and freighters, and winced back from the sound. He was past his saloon, heading south toward the Buffum's house, when he heard someone shout in the roadway and turned in time to see the lean, tall man with the carbine step into some watery light, raise the gun toward him and fire. But Troy had ample time. He moved sideways with deceptive speed, swearing and tearing at his coat, palming the derringer helplessly, knowing it was no match—ever—for a long-gun.

The slug shot up a gyrating splinter ten inches long from the fir duckboards where he had been standing, then someone was calling his name. He heard men erupting from the saloon, yelling to one another in half drunken excitement.

The astonishment of being a target held him flat against the inner wall of a store, weak-kneed after his first fright had passed, and amazed. It didn't make sense. He assumed he had enemies because of his new wealth, but he knew of no reason why anyone would want to kill him. Not even Jeb, the only man he knew who wouldn't hesitate to snuff out a life. Tom Buffum's words came back. He heard them once more in his mind; but it just wasn't like the sheriff. No—this was something else.

He risked a glance. To his amazement, the rifleman was coming down the middle of the road, shouting his name, roaring challenges and curses. He held the saddle gun hip high, cocked and highlighted in dull silver by every small passageway of fallen light.

Troy's uncertainty turned to self preservation. There was no way out of the cul-de-sac between the buildings, unless he went forward. He did. Like a maddened bull, knowing he had to close the gap fast in order for the little gun to be effective. He came out light on his feet and fast, the derringer cocked and held high and outward. Just one thing saved him. Tom Buffum was running back uptown from the direction of his house. He had his pistol out, cocked and riding evenly in his fist, when he cried out.

"You there! You with that carbine! Throw her down—damn you!"

The lean, tall man swung his head back to Troy as the little .41 exploded. He staggered backwards under impact, squeezed the carbine's trigger, recoiled again, and never heard the second thunderous crash of the

45

derringer because it was too close, and he was falling forward, slowly, reluctantly, as though his deadened mind knew, once down, he'd never arise. He never would, either. Troy's first shot had torn a hole in his chest half as large as a dinner plate.

"Troy! Throw that damned gun down!"

The little gun went into the dust near the scarlet pool that was being avidly drunk up by the dry earth. Troy's eyes were staring over the dead gunman at Tom.

"Who the hell is he, Tom?"

The sheriff holstered his gun with a savage, bitter gesture. He didn't answer, but knelt, rolled the man on to his back and saw the dirt that adhered to the curly, thick black hair and wide, blue eyes, then he straightened, looking across at Troy again.

"How'd it happen, Troy?"

"Don't know—exactly. I was walking down the plankwalk there. I heard someone—him maybe—call out my name. I turned and there he was, bringing the carbine up and aiming at me. I ducked between two buildings. He—must have been crazy, Tom. Good God—he just levered the gun and kept coming." Troy's dark eyes went over the handsome, dead face. "Never saw the damned fool before in my life, Tom. That I know of."

"You didn't, huh." Tom's face was like granite. Each line softened under the nightlight, but the cold eyes and rocky chin standing out rock-hard and unforgiving.

"No. Who is he? You know?"

Tom nodded. "Sure. His name's Will Jennings. He's from over at Herd's Crossing."

The shock came in and struck him hard behind the eyes. Jennings! Of course! It was clear—painfully, bitterly clear. Cin had run to her lover. Jennings—the man he had

46

smilingly told himself was a fool for loving his wife—had come down to Bannock to kill him, and there he lay; dead with both Troy's .41 slugs in his body.

Troy lifted an ashen face, saw Tom watching him, used every remaining ounce of resourcefulness he still had, to force up a shrug that was supposed to indicate indifference but didn't fool the sheriff at all, then he turned slowly, heavily, like an old man, and walked slowly back on to the duckboards and south again, eyes wide open and unseeing when he passed the Buffum house. Still wide open and blank with horror, when the plankwalk ran out and the rangeland began, far beyond the tarpaper shacks. He didn't stop until he was at the foot of the old oak, then he let himself down, lay back with his head cradled on his big hands, and looked up at the clear night, allowing the entire sordidness that had followed his first handclasp with Jeb Carter, to walk slowly, ponderously, across his mind's eye.

He hadn't been there so long before Ellie moved out of the obscurity of the night and looked down at him. She had seen him go by. Recognized the shock in the way he went, and followed him. Instinct told her most of what had happened, the cries of men farther up town had filled in the rest.

"Troy. Oh, Troy."

She knelt and watched his dark eyes come around to her slowly, distantly, seeing her, looking past and through her and beyond at the night again. She put a hand on his face. It was cold. He blinked at the touch, sat up suddenly and shook his head like a stunned bull.

"Ellie—you shouldn't have come here."

"No, and you shouldn't have either. Who—was he?"

"Hombre named Jennings. Will Jennings."

"I don't know him," she said with evident relief.

47

"Why did he try to kill you?"

"Over Cin. I never saw the man before in my life. Cin's been seeing him for a long time. I knew about it, Ellie."

"You didn't care?"

He shook his head at her. "I—don't know whether I did or not—up until we kissed, before. I honestly don't know. Now, of course, I don't give a darn. Only—I didn't want to kill him."

"Of course not, Troy." She was silent for a while, still kneeling, but letting her hand fall to his lap where it lay softly upon his own great paw. "Did—Tom see you tonight?"

He raised his head and saw the luminousness of her eyes. "Yes; he came by earlier. Told me not to see you again."

"What did you say?"

"That I'd let you decide whether we'd see each other—or not."

She didn't follow the line of his conversation. She switched over quickly and fluidly to what was uppermost in her mind. "Troy—stop it. All of it. Give Carter back his saloon."

"I tried to, tonight, Ellie. He—we—decided to wait until the end of the year."

"No," she said with a soft toss of her head. "You can't. You just can't go on like this until the end of the year. Troy—it'll ruin everything. May even—cause your death. Worse—it'll wreck every shred of what we have found together, again. Do it now, Troy. Now—tonight or tomorrow."

He felt the hardness within him that had grown so insidiously over the past months, arise and stiffen his resolve again. The dead man's face was obliterated by it completely.

"All right, darnit. But—Jeb won't be back until next week sometime."

She touched his upper arm, let her hand stay high and fiercely possessive, when she moved closer, peering into his face. "You'll do it, Troy? You'll break with Carter for good, when he comes back? Your word?"

The intentness in her look, posture and voice made him smile down at her. "My word, my darling. Sealed with a kiss."

She surrendered completely then, lying against him unashamed, fighting with every ounce of control to keep from crying, letting the agony in her heart well over until she knew she'd have to cry, then buried her face against the rough, tobacco smelling cloth of his coat, and gave over the battle so that, when the dam broke, Troy was startled by its awful intensity, and held her closer, trying to still the cries and absorb the anguish that racked her body, with his own great bulk.

CHAPTER FOUR

BUT JEB CARTER HAD OTHER IDEAS. HE DRANK RYE whiskey and sat across from Troy like a lean, tawny wolf. The chilled blue eyes showed his soul beyond, impaled on spikes of inner ferocity. He shook his head.

"No, by gawd. Not after you killed Jennings. He was the only alternative I had, Troy."

Troy's dark glance was dull. He felt constricting fingers entwining his heart, imprisoning him within a jail of his own making. He knew it would be like this, and worse, so long as he stayed a partner to this ruthless renegade. Knew also, that everything he had done for

49

the past half a year, had been wrong. Everything. And the bearded man across the room from him was the reason—that, and a foolish fear he'd held, once, that he might lose Cin, a woman who had never loved him anyway—who couldn't ever love anyone—and that too, was wrong, immature sort of, because now he knew, inside himself, that he did not love her at all. With the coming of his trials had also come maturity. It had brought something with it that made these things glaringly clear, now.

"No Jeb. This is my last night here. Listen—"

"No," Carter said quietly. "You listen. Have you bought into the stage line yet?"

"Yeah. Week ago. This Jennings was the line's Herd's Crossing manager. That was another blunder of mine. Campbell was put out about me killing him."

"I reckon," Jeb said drily. "But that's not our problem. What matters to me is that you stay on here. Six months, anyway."

Troy saw the danger signals running up in the lean, hard face, and pushed blindly ahead in spite of them. "I can't do it, Jeb. I'm sorry."

"Damn you," Carter said with no inflection in his voice, just a mounting irritation. "You've made more money than you knew existed. You're spreading out now and getting respectable. Well, don't think you'll use me for your stepping stone, Troy. No one's done it yet."

"Jeb, it isn't that. I'll give you my share of the Palace—of the money. The stage line, too, if you want it."

"I wouldn't want to own an interest in a stage line," the outlaw said drily, pouring himself another shot of whiskey.

50

"I'll still have the money I got from the sale of the blacksmith shop. Enough to get started in something else—somewhere—and you're welcome to the rest, but—Jeb—I won't be around here after tonight."

Carter ran the back of a hand across his mouth, combed at the hair with crooked fingers and pinpointed Troy with his steady, baleful glare.

"I don't know what's got into you. Don't give a curse. Maybe it's that woman of your's. Well—don't cross me, Troy. Don't cross me!"

Troy's big head came up a little. "What about—my wife?" He started to lean forward in his chair, ready to get up, then hesitated looking at the outlaw. "What do you mean?"

Carter appraised the huge expanse of shoulders; the great thickness of chest, and let one hand drop away to his side. He shrugged. "Well—let's say you threw her out. That's good enough. Anyway, you got her so damned riled she's trying to hire someone to kill you."

"You know where she is?"

"Sure; Herd's Crossing." Carter was surprised at Troy's look of scorn. Briefly, his own ruthlessness had been willing to kill this man—in self-defence—who was his mainstay in the Palace Bar. He figured it might happen over mention of Troy's wife, but he had chanced it in the hope that he could influence Troy to stay on and manage the saloon, Dead, Troy Muller was less use to him than anything. The silence between them grew.

Troy eased back slowly in his chair, lost in the bitterness of Carter's revelation. His wife, whom he'd once thought the finest woman in the world, was out for her final revenge.

His head went back slowly. He chuckled, letting the sound come out deep and heavy until it arose into a laugh and died away again as his head came down. He regarded the staring outlaw with irony. Perhaps Jeb had been with Cin. She was the type who would appeal strongly to a hunted, affection starved man like Carter. He would be another one fooled—and tortured—by her beauty—and her hatred. It didn't mean a thing, except that she would tantalize him even more. Add weight to whose ever shoulders she was with.

Troy smiled softly, ironically. It occurred to him that he felt no pain at the full knowledge of what Cin had done—was doing. In fact, there was a shade of relief in his mind. Relief and sardonic amusement.

"She sicked Jennings on me, Jeb. I know that. She's trying again?"

A nod, short, brusque and granite hard. The blue eyes were wide and steady, and not understanding Troy Muller at all.

Troy grunted, letting his face smooth over into stony blankness. "Whoever wants her can have her."

Jeb shrugged. "Listen; if you'll stay on for six months more I'll bring her back, hogtied, and make you a present of her.'"

"To the devil with her."

Carter was silent a moment, then he got up slowly. Troy read the signs aright and arose also, going around his desk until scarcely two feet separated them. He was unafraid even though he knew he was no match for the killer. That the little gun in his coat was useless—might just as well have been at home in the bureau drawer—for all the good it could do him in a showdown with Jeb.

The gunman's face was pinched tight with emotion. He was standing perfectly erect, no hint of a crouch or a stoop to him, when he spoke again.

"Troy—you got a choice. The Palace, or—wherever

in hades you sent Jennings!"

Troy smiled and the blunt, rocky expanse of his face was made extremely unpleasant by the look. "Well—maybe Jennings wasn't such a bad hombre, in a lot of ways; after all. He was a fool, but—" He was catapulted through the air by the tremendous power in his large legs. Jeb Carter swore once in an explosive, startled, livid voice and streaked for his gun. They went down together, half over Carter's chair, knocking the whiskey bottle to the floor from impact, then Troy's big hands were doubled in fury and raining blows into the sinewy hard body that kicked free with the agility of a desperate eel and staggered for footing.

Troy came up not quite so fast as the leaner, lighter man, but still fast enough to rattle Carter's aim when his gun went off with a thunderous explosion that rocked the office and made their ears ring.

As though by prearranged signal the saloon's furor beyond the office door died out in a pall of silence, then men were pounding on the panel crying out Troy's name. Jeb scarcely heard them as he flung a kick at Troy's stomach, missed by inches and received Troy's boot solidly. He doubled forward in spite of a gasping effort not to, then Troy was after him with great, sledgehammer blows that should have felled the lesser man.

Carter dropped his right hand gun, the only one he still clutched, went to his knees in retrieving it and thus missed two vicious blows that, had they landed, would have finished him. He went sideways, like a crab, for three shuffling steps, then raised quickly and flung himself through the open window.

Troy heard the body fall against the packed ground, rise and hurry off. The sound of the killer's spur rowers

53

made an incongruous melody of sound as an aftermath.

He was still standing in the wreckage of the office when the door burst inward and both his night barmen were standing there, six-guns in one fist and wagon spokes, the saloonman's standby, clutched in their opposite fists. Troy lifted an arm that ached and motioned them away, seeing the wild eyed looks they wore.

"All over, boys. Forget it."

He went over ponderously, wearily, and closed the broken door in their astonished faces and leaned against it, hearing the sounds come back into the bar-room, then there was a single shot outside—then another with a fast second explosion. He crossed the room with wonder etched in his features. Jeb must have stumbled into someone outside his window who recognized and challenged him. Cautiously, he peered out the window. There was nothing there he could see but—but—

It was an icicle of fear that dropped down out of memory and stayed with him as he vaulted through the opening and went forward to the prone, lumpy thing he knew was a body. It couldn't be—shouldn't be—but it was!

Tom Buffum!

The big man's anguish rose up inside of him as he knelt by the sodden form, looking down at it in real fear—almost in prayerful supplication—until he rolled the sheriff over and saw his face. There were two bloody stains on his clothing. One, high and to the right in his chest, made the butternut shirt sticky and black looking in the darkness. The other was somewhere below the belt and to the left, in Tom's thigh. Almost sick with misgivings, Troy explored the chest wound. He knew what had happened even though Buffum

54

couldn't tell him. It was simple now, but an hour before he never would have considered it. And that was another mistake because he distinctly remembered what Tom had told him at the boarding house.

"The first chance I get to nail either one of you, or both, I'm going to do it."

He made a pad of his handkerchief and lay it over the wound, then stood up. There was a gleam of hope in his dark eyes—faintly—when he turned away, walking hurriedly down the alley toward the doctor's house, trying to remember a prayer from somewhere in his life, and failing. Thinking only of how Tom had staked out his office and met Jeb Carter coming out. He thought ruefully, too, that if Jeb had gone his usual, leisurely way, Torn would have gotten him. Which was another wrong directly attributable to Troy, for he had started the fight that had launched Carter through the window like a cannonball—and inadvertently saved the outlaw's life, and likely had cost Ellie's brother his own.

He was thinking of Ellie's face all the time he spoke to the doctor, telling him where the sheriff was. When the medical man left the house, mumbling through clenched teeth and jerking at a reluctant arm of his coat, Troy went back out on to the duckboards, bareheaded, disheveled, his torn coat and shirt stained with blood, and walked blindly south through Bannock.

If there was a way to tell a woman her brother was close to death—if not dead—without paralyzing her with horror, Troy's mind failed to find it in its groping, desperate search for a way to say what he brought with him to tell Ellie.

He saw with a vague, foggy perspective, the startled, horrified looks that went by him as he walked, and ignored them until he was in front of the Buffum cottage. Here, he shoved the bloody shirt back into his trousers, ran shaking fingers through his hair and knocked on the door. The V in his throat was pulsating unevenly, erratically, and the shock in his eyes was writhing, back in the depths.

Ellie saw him that way when she opened the door and looked out. Alarm came instantly into her face. "Troy—what in the name?—Are you hurt?"

She was reaching for him, tugging at one thick, limp arm, pulling him into the house, eyes going shades darker in instant apprehension.

"Ellie; it—it isn't me, honey. Sit down—I—"

"Tom!" The way her intuition flashed up the name and the way it was torn out of her sent pain through him as tangible as any he'd ever felt.

"Tom? Is it—Tom—Troy?"

He nodded down at the imploring look.

"It's Tom, Ellie. Jeb Carter shot him behind the Palace. In the alley. The doctor's with him. I—went there before I came down here."

"He isn't dead, Troy?"

He fought back the desperate desire to say what she wanted him to say. Tom hadn't been dead when Troy had left him. She read the reservations in his eyes before he answered, and lightened her grip on his upper arms.

"No."

She shook him then, by the arms, until he locked his teeth against the pain of fingernails going through his coat like pointed teeth.

"Troy! Will he live. Is it bad?"

He never answered. Never had the chance to. She whirled away from him and lunged toward the door. He was left standing there, watching her, when spurred boots and deep, muffled sounds of men's voices raised

56

and yet low and soft, came from the walkway beyond the house. He watched in fascination as Ellie threw the door open and stood limned in the opening, the lantern light behind her outlining the intent, thrust-forward way she was holding her head, staring out into the night. A shaft of cold air swept across his face when the men came in, four of them, carrying Tom in a grimy old blanket, the doctor beside the stricken, lolling form of Tom Buffum.

Ellie ran ahead of them, slammed open the sheriff's bedroom door and disappeared inside with the men. Troy felt immense, ill at ease and out of place. He felt all the acute guilt a man must, under the circumstances. He could have prevented it—but how? He had no inkling the sheriff would lie in ambush outside his office window, and yet he might have suspected it. Tom Buffum was an open book to Troy Muller. He was a persistent, doggedly valorous man, tolerant and humorous and thoroughly likable—nevertheless everyone knew too, that he was also a confirmed lawman.

He was still standing there, conscious of his damaged clothing, bruised flesh and futility, and scourging himself with the knowledge of dilemma and the fact that, should Tom be dead—or die—he would lose Ellie as surely as though he had shot her brother down himself, when the doctor came out of the room followed by the four cowboys, who trouped awkwardly on tiptoe to the door and went back out into the night.

He could hear the sounds of Ellie's sobs in the next room and looked at the doctor. Once more his tongue was plank-like against the roof of his mouth. He didn't recognize his voice, either, when it came out.

"Is he dead, doc?"

57

The plume of white hair wagged once negatively. The gray eyes showed no friendliness. "No; not yet."

"Will he die?"

"The Lord knows—I don't!" The words snapped out irritably while the gray eyes stayed on Troy's face savagely. "Muller—I hope you're satisfied!"

"What do you mean?"

"Just what I said. It's none of my business—naturally—but, there are times when it's difficult not to express an opinion. All Bannock knows about you. Not just about your saloon, your wife—and other things. but about you and Tom—and Ellie." The white thatch bobbed brusquely. "Well—I hope you're satisfied with what else you've done to this girl—now!"

Troy's fists were clenched. He said nothing and it is doubtful if the doctor would have stopped long enough to listen anyway. He turned short and went back toward the wounded man's room, his back erect and inflexible, as defiant and outraged and eloquent as it could be.

Troy was moving toward the door when he heard the sound of Ellie's skirts behind him. He turned slowly, raising his eyes with their ill look. She came up close to him, the passing of every tear like a scar on her face.

"Troy—he's conscious. He—wants you."

"Ellie—" He raised one limp, massive hand and let it fall again.

She stopped him with a look. "Don't. Just go in and see him." She turned and walked swiftly toward the kitchen where hot water was in the kettle on the wood, range. Hot water and clean rags.

Troy went back across the parlor until he was at Tom's doorway, then he entered, looking down at the ashen face with its blue lips and feverish, lusterless eyes that moved so tiredly to his face and clung there, groping until recognition came, then lighted up a little.

"Troy? He—sure can shoot—can't he?"

The doctor ignored the stalwart bulk beside the bed and worked with pursed lips and smoldering eyes.

Troy nodded. "I reckon, Tom. The—son of a b . . ."

"I—heard some of it, Troy. Not all—of it though. I—was going away when—the fight started. You—and Jeb. Going—after somebody—to deputize—when the ruckus started."

"You came back, Tom, in time to run into him on the way out?"

"Yeah. Got off—one shot. He got off—two. Good shooting, too. He was—hurt—and running—and it was dark as hell."

"That'll be enough, Tom." The cold tones cut into Troy like iron slivers dipped in venom. He glanced once at the baleful look on the doctor's face, and bent down a little.

"Tom; listen to me. You just said you were going after someone to deputize to help you get him. Well—all right—here's your man."

Buffum stared up into the dark eyes over his bed. He could see the anguish in them easily enough. He blinked a couple of times. They both heard Ellie come back into the room with the vessel of hot water, and ignored her. Tom made a microscopic movement with his head, like an infinitesimal nod, then he tried to smile. It took a lot of effort and wasn't more than a third successful, but Troy understood.

"All right, Troy." The words were weak, slow and grave. Even the doctor straightened, watching the drama, and Ellie, in the background, had one hand at her throat. Then it was over and Tom glanced toward his bureau.

"Top—right hand drawer, Troy. Damned—deputy's badge."

While Troy was after the badge, Tom's eyes swept over the big man with a knowing look and he spoke again. "Troy? Help me get this gun off. It's—goddamned heavy on me—now." When the gunbelt and gun were dangling in Troy's hands, Tom looked up at him steadily. "No sense—hanging it on a chair, deputy. Buckle it around—you. You'll need it—and maybe ten more like it—before you—run him down."

Troy's smile was bitterly understanding as he donned the sheriff's armament. He nodded. "I reckon, Tom. I—reckon. Well—" he turned and found the doctor's expression relenting a triffle, not quite so hostile now. "If I knew how to pray, Doc—but I don't. I got lots of faith in you—don't let any of us down, will you?"

"I'm not a miracle man," the doctor said testily, but the gray eyes were paying a small tribute to Troy, in spite of the curt words. "You take care of your end of things—deputy—and I'll take care of mine."

Troy glanced over at Ellie. She was staring at him with circlets of blue under each eyes and a thin, white strip over her upper lip where she was fighting back the agony that made her throat feel like it was red hot. He was afraid to speak to her. Afraid even to look up at her, for long: so he brushed silently past, face downcast and devastatingly conscious of her nearness and the magnetic pull that made him want to glance back, just once, then he was out in the parlor again and striding toward the door.

The night was like before. Black and scratchy with homely sounds. Troy was past the front gate when the voice reached out for him.

"Troy."

He turned and watched her come down the plankwalk from the house, saying nothing. Letting the immense surge of emotion overwhelm him temporarily, then grinding it back and letting his dark eyes see her oval face, pale in the gloom and close to his own across the little gate.

"Troy; what can I say to stop you? I love you so very, very much, and he'll kill you, my darling. You're no gunfighter. God in Heaven, Troy—don't go after him. I—couldn't lose you again—and Tom too. I—just couldn't!"

He bent down and kissed her hair where the moonlight, weak and watery as it was, made crescents of light among the waves.

"Ellie; I don't know how to say what I feel. It's sort of like this. Carter's not wholly at fault. I am—mostly. It's been like this—ever since I went into partnership with him. I've made wrong moves one after another all this year—almost. I'm the one that's got these bad debts, honey. I'm the one that's got to pay 'em off. It's—almost like his money's evil—or something. There's only this one way, darling. Face Carter."

"No! Troy, listen to me; he's a killer. A—"

"I know all that. He's more than a killer. He's a lot of things you never heard of. It doesn't change a thing. The point is, Ellie, I led Tom into this. By being blind, like you told me I was. Well, now I've got to settle it, make these amends. Tom can't, you can't and Carter can't. But I can. I've got to, Ellie."

"Troy darling, believe me. It's already done. Tom's shot. Another man dying won't solve a thing."

"It isn't that. That's what I'm trying to tell you. It's a whole lot of things that I'm responsible for. Tom's only one of 'em. The final one, maybe, but still only one.

Please, Ellie," he reached over the gate and took her shoulders in his big hands, holding her that way, motionless and inches away, looking into her face, a sad, chastened man who had come a long way, up hill and down—a lifetime of inner growth, in fact—in less than a year. From a blacksmith shop with an easy going, passive nature; a certain stolidness; to the Palace Bar and subsequent affluence, and the hardness that had grown on him during that time, to where he stood now, scarred forever on his soul by the initial mistake that forged him anew after Tom's shooting, and made him stare at Ellie like that.

"It's kind of like that story they told us about in school where those folks had to pay the piper, whether they wanted to or not." His hands pulled her up against the gate convulsively.

"And remember this, Ellie; I love you, girl. So much it hurts, and I'm sorry for the past—sorry about Cin and other things—and I'll come back to you as soon as I can, darling."

"If you can," she said softly, searching for his mouth. "You mean—if you can, Troy; God!"

He kissed her in the subdued stillness of the night, feeling a poignancy he'd never felt before, letting all the sorrow out at once, to mix with the crucible fire that burned steadily in him for her, and breathing inwardly, deeply, fixing the scent of lavender that clung to her, eternally in his mind. Then he moved away, forcing his eyes to leave her and went slowly up the duckboards toward Sweeney's liverybarn, on the north side of what had once been Muller's Forge; the shop in Bannock where he'd started from.

The rest of the night was a dimly recalled torture, in later years. Sweeney's startled face and popping eyes when Troy'd taken the horse, paid in advance and told him he'd better collect while he could. Swinging aboard and striking out over the north road leading to Herd's Crossing. A faint, tortured trail that meandered into the uplands and flung itself across the undulating land like a harassed snake, and wound along in the darkness with its lone traveler, a big man on a sturdy, chesty sorrel gelding, riding slouched and grim and wraith like, resembling a phantom man on a phantom horse.

The first knife blade shaft of pink was ripping into the soft underbelly of the swollen blackness when Troy broke over a landswell and saw Herd's Crossing far off. A faint, geometrical pattern of upright shadows growing gray and unearthly looking, lighter against the bolder, dark cold of a false dawn.

He rode with no plan in mind except one. To kill a man. How he would accomplish this, where or when, were all small facets of an unknown whole. He didn't think of them until he was shuffling along through the deathly grayness, into the roadway of Herd's Crossing, seeing the mongrel dogs, slab-sided, nosing in the manure behind the hitchrails and through the dust beside the deserted plankwalks, and hearing roosters sounding off into the teeth of a new day.

At the liverybarn, Troy stepped down, paid in advance for the horse's keep—stalled and grained— then glanced at the hostler skeptically, knowing the man for the slops drinking brotherhood he belonged to.

"Where can a man get breakfast?"

The nighthawk had already appraised the dull, fixed look of the dark eyes, the thonged down gun and the powerful build of the stranger, and decided—gunman. Lifting an emaciated arm inside a filthy sleeve, he pointed across the bleak roadway.

"Yonder's a beanery. Beat on the door. Cookie lives in back."

Troy walked, hearing the echo of his own spurs in the stillness of the Crossing. He read the sign and struck the door like it was an enemy. The old man who let him in was puffy eyed and hadn't put his teeth in yet. He was wrinkled and worn with the elements and the years on a frontier that had even less to offer, in his era, than it had now.

"Java, cowboy?"

"I reckon. That, and bacon and ham, if you got 'em." Troy eased his weary, cold frame down on to the bench that ran along in front of the counter.

"Oh heck," the old man said with a downward, contemptuous twist of his toothless, moist lips. "I always got that stuff. Always, boy. 'Low me a minute or two to rassle it up. Light up a shuck, boy, and sit back."

Troy blinked at the man's breeziness, seeming indifference. Fishing around, he found his tobacco sack and made a deliberate, perfect cigarette, mouthed it and inhaled. The smoke went all the way to his toes and made a mild rush of dizziness fog inside his mind. He hadn't smoked in fifteen and more hours. That memory annoyed him, too. Everything had changed—or stopped—since Tom had been shot down. Everything. Even his habits, his thoughts, almost, and his bearing. There was a void inside of him that was surrounded by determination to kill a man; nothing else.

He longed for a spot to sit and sift his thoughts. Idly, while the odors of frying meat overcame the older, ranker smells of Herd's Crossing, he went back over it all again. The total came out as it had before.

Troy's bad alliance was first, then it went down fast, like a plummet. The money he'd acquired. An alarming

64

amount of it considering the short space of time involved. He had made every decision—as a businessman—correctly. For the woman who had been his wife, he had done these things. To hold her. Another, deeper step downward into turmoil, then. She had left him—hated him now so unreasoningly, she was offering everything to any man who would kill him.

Another run downward into degradation. He had—inadvertently or not didn't matter—led Tom to the gates of death, and Ellie—to suffering such as one woman shouldn't know in a lifetime.

And across this mental ledger, was the other deficit column. The one that showed every move he'd made since he'd paired off with Jeb Carter, as a human being, to be wrong. Brought anguish to those he cared the most for, sacrificed his self respect to the townsmen—like the doctor, for instance—and now found himself at the end of the trail. In the unenviable situation where atonement wouldn't ever erase all that was inscribed against him on the slate, and yet he had to try to make amends in a way that was synonymous with suicide. All—because he had been weak, once, over what he had thought, then, was a good cause, and which had turned to be—nothing.

It all went through his mind slowly, almost pleasantly like pure logic usually does, so that by the time the old man called Cookie, brought in his breakfast, floating in a coating of grease that would adhere to the top of his mouth for the balance of the day, he had an almost pleasant feeling in his mind, of knowing exactly why he was in Herd's Crossing, and what he must do before he left the place—vertical or horizontal.

He smiled slowly, sardonically, at the man. "Cookie; you know the boys hereabouts?"

"I expect, boy. Been around the Crossing for close to

forty years. Used to guide for Crook's army when they was In'yuns all over these darned hills and prairies."

"Known a lot of hard ones in your day, eh?"

"My share." Cookie's eyes were going cautious in his study of the powerful man across the counter from him. "You—looking for someone?"

"Yeah. Someone. Don't expect you could tell me where I could find him, though."

"Dunno. Dunno. You could try."

Another sardonic smile from Troy as he watched caution become solid and graceless on the old, wrinkled, ugly face.

"Feller named Jeb Carter."

"Nope; can't help you, boy." It came out almost before Troy had stopped speaking. The words ran into each other so that it sounded like one prolonged, compound word. "Can't he'p you a-tall, there, boy. Sorry."

Troy grunted around his food without looking up. "Nothing to be sorry about, oldtimer. There'll be folks hereabouts who'll know where I can find him. Ought to be anyway. Carter said he hung around Herd's Crossing."

"You—know him? A friend of his?"

"More'n that, Cookie; he and I are partners."

There was a silence so long and loud it was like an earache. Cookie didn't budge away from his cake table. Just leaned on it staring off over Troy's head, out the open door and beyond the town itself, down the years, possibly.

"Used to be a lot of outlaws around the Crossing."

"I expect," Troy said, eating slower now, savoring the food that he wanted so badly for so long without being aware of his hunger until be sat down to eat.

"Yeah; lots of 'em." The sunken eyes came down to Troy's face, studied it carefully, as though he meant to describe it later, maybe, then the bony shoulders rose and fell silently.

"Tell you what, cowboy. When you're through here, go down to Slattery's Saloon. It's at the far south end of town. Ask around down there. Might be some of the boys could help you, I don't know. Just a guess, sort of, y'know."

"Sure," Troy said, looking up guardedly at the old man and wondering what would be in the memories of such a man as he. Old and left behind by his violent generation. Probably more violence than he could imagine. "I'll do that. Slattery's."

"Yeah; Slattery's Saloon. South end of town."

CHAPTER FIVE

BUT SLATTERY'S SALOON HAD A HEAVILY PADLOCKED panel behind the louvered doors that was as forbidding and formidable as it was deterring to Troy's quest.

He stared out over the lifeless town wondering what to do with himself until the saloon opened, and decided he didn't like Herd's Crossing any more now than when he'd first seen it years before.

It was a functional cowtown, unkempt, worn smooth with the passage of many booted feet, scarred along the baseboards where spurs had gouged the wood for time out of mind, when lounging riders—and outlaws—had kept lazy vigils on tilted-back chairs, from beneath the warped, peeling overhead wooden awnings, and he couldn't see a single shred of beauty to the place, anywhere—for the simple reason that there wasn't any.

"Mornin' stranger."

Troy turned, saw the compact figure behind him with the tentative smile and appraising, faded blue eyes above a sharply hooked nose, and nodded. The man lounged over a little closer. A dull reflection of light slapped, once, against the nickel star inside a circlet of the same metal on his shirt. Troy raked him over with a glance and saw the gun, tied down and efficient looking, that hung close to a thick, short leg.

"Morning, Constable."

"Ain't I seen you before, partner?"

Troy shrugged, irritated a little. "Maybe. I'm from Bannock."

"Yeah." the constable said slowly, still smiling but obviously using the expression to hide some mental labors designed to dredge up recognition of the big man.

"Town's still abed, from the looks of things; ain't it?"

Troy nodded. "Looks that way. What time's Slattery's open up."

The constable's faded eyes flickered over the padlocked door when he shrugged, musingly. "Oh. They might open up about an hour or so from now. Hard to say." He smiled again. "Depends on how long they was open last night, I expect."

"Yeah," Troy said dourly, "I expect." He turned abruptly away and stalked back down toward the liverybarn. It annoyed him the way the constable stared, smiled his wolfish, blank grin, and made clever remarks.

The hostler blinked at him and nodded. "Get fed?"

"Yeah. Saddle me a horse. I'll ride around until this graveyard comes to life." He didn't say there was a nagging premonition inside of him, making him restless. He watched the man start toward the horse he had ridden to Herd's Crossing and shook his head at him.

"No; a livery horse. That one's earned a rest."

When the animal—a massive, stolid bay with a Roman-nose—was brought up and saddled, Troy swung up, nodded curtly and reined out into the drab roadway, swung north through town until he saw a side-road leading west, took it indifferently and let the ugly bay horse pick his own route and pace.

There was something inside of him that was working in a roil of turmoil; nagging for movement, driving him to keep moving. It was an uneasy sensation, and foreign to him.

He rode along old cow trails until he broke over a long, rolling rib of land left behind by some ancient ocean on its march down the land to the sea, and reined up. Behind and below, lay Herd's Crossing, so named because of the two tortured, wavering old wagon roads that came out of nowhere, crossed at the town's northern limits, and wound blindly on again, into Eternity.

He made a cigarette, cupped his hand, lit it and smoked. Somewhere, probably not too far away either, Cin was thinking of him. He was sure of it. Jeb would have told her, more than likely, of their disagreement. He wondered idly if it was some telepathic warning from her angry, vengeful mind, that prompted his feeling to ride away from the Crossing?

He shrugged, spat over the hand holding the cigarette and let narrowed, brooding eyes wander over the great upland expanse of land where, in the cold, far reaches, sentinel pines and firs cloaked the higher foothills and peaks, purple and somber looking. A lift of the reins and a nudge, and the bay horse went on again.

The animal seemed almost as indifferent as his rider. He moved placidly enough, and only an experienced

69

rider would have known that he had a destination in mind as he went due west, angling a little toward the closest fringe of shadowy looking forest. Troy understood and let him go. It didn't make any difference—he thought.

The trees weren't far ahead and the sun was climbing steadily, hotly, searching for victims to dehydrate; exact pitiful and full payment in sweat, from man and beast who had to toil over the dry land under the searing whiplash of its fury.

Troy considered turning back. He knew Slattery's would be open by now but the shade of the nearing forest looked too inviting. He let the bay horse go, figuring a nap in the shade would make him feel better.

The sun was relaxing the tight muscles in his back, burning evenly through his shirt and warming him until he slouched, sinking into a sort of weariness inspired drowsiness. What brought him out of it was the sound of loping horses behind, on his back trail. Frowning, he reined up, twisted and looked back. A peculiar sensation clutched his stomach. There were two horsemen coming toward him, heads bent over his tracks as they rode, and both had their saddle guns lying across their laps. It wasn't for convenience sake either, for both men had saddle boots strapped under the fenders. They were out to kill and they were tracking him.

He cursed and swung back just as one of the pursuers raised his head, saw him and raised a cry that was blood chilling and triumphant, both. He hung in the spurs, felt the bay gather himself mightily, then leap wildly forward and land running.

The forest wasn't more than a mile ahead. He rode low, watching it come up on his rough gaited horizon, seeking a path, an opening—anything—that would permit his mounted passage. There were a lot of places he could ride through, but few that showed any previous travel.

A carbine roared behind him. Teeth clenched, he darted a backward glance and saw the men were gaining. There was no use to spur the ugly bay any more. He was running his best, whether it was good enough or not. Troy swore, pulled his .45 and held it, waiting for the range to lessen, knowing that when it did, he'd probably be dead anyway. The trees were close now. He twisted, let fly a high one in the hope of at least inspiring caution in his pursuers, and flung himself low when a fusillade answered his wasted shot.

At first, there was just the sensation of being struck across the back, and no pain. He was sure it was a limb he'd failed to see as the forest swallowed up his bay horse, then a wave of shock passed over his mind. The shoulder of his shirt was slimy and warm. He had been hit! Fury boiled up inside of him. There was no escape anyway. The bay horse had served him to the best of its ability. He reined up suddenly, jerking the Roman-nose back so far it was almost in his lap, swung down and flung the reins around the saddlehorn. Two searching shots inspired activity in the animal. It went away, quartering the place like it was on familiar ground, then disappeared among the trees.

In the gloom and coolness of the forest, Troy hunkered beside a rotting old deadfall, waiting. His eyes were like black ice, and vicious. There could be only one explanation to this chase. Either Cookie, back at the cafe in Herd's Crossing, or the town constable, had passed the word along to Carter. No one else in Herd's Crossing would want him badly enough to hire men to kill him. He squinted at the plain beyond, searching for the men or their horses, and seeing neither.

It had to be Cookie. He was the only man in town that knew who Troy was after. He smiled to himself and shook his head. Another mistake! Maybe fatal, this time. Well—if he ever got back . . . A blue jay screamed sudden, startled defiance somewhere off to his right. He knew one of the men, perhaps both, were coming down toward him. He settled lower, feeling the oily stickiness of sweat on his face, and resting the cocked hand-gun across the old dead trunk.

There was a rhythmic, pulsating sense of mild pain in his back that came and went with each heartbeat. He longed to change positions so that he could explore the wound, but was afraid to do so. A snapped twig, a blur of movement, and he would be in jeopardy. Death was out there somewhere, stalking him with two sets of deadly eyes.

But Troy never heard or felt it when it came. Just a flash of incredible brilliance, dazzling, searing and benumbing all at once.

He never knew that the blue jay left in swooping, frantic flight when the explosion erupted and chased the echoes out through the trees and beyond. He didn't feel the gloved fist that yanked him off his side, plucked at him with brutal indifference until he was face up, claret spilling out of his mouth, over the edge of his lips and mixing with the leaf mold, and running down into the V of his neck and pouring inside his shirt. He didn't hear one man speak, either.

"That's it. Let's get the devil out of here."

The tall, cadaverous, hawkfaced man with one eye and dark brown stains in either corner of his slash of a mouth, grunted, flicked the blood off his glove, grasped his carbine tighter and turned away.

"Yeah. That was a quick hundred."

"Not easy though—dammit."

"No," hawkface said, moving away abruptly. "But you'll get used to it, kid. All right; let's go collect."

They went. The one-eyed man leading the way, his spurless boots clumping carelessly over the dry wood and leaves; his savage face twisted up, still, with the tenseness that uncoiled slowly inside of him.

As far as Troy was concerned, there was just oblivion. He not only didn't exist as a man, but he wasn't even an intelligence. Not until he opened his eyes and felt a certain stumbling, retarded sort of mental functioning going on within his head that was full of bewilderment, fever and pain.

There was a sooty ceiling over him and a smell of greasy food that made his stomach writhe, then he was looking into a scored, sere old face with a week's growth of beard stubble on it, and two skeptical, wise old eyes that were neither brown or blue, but rather a kind of hazel-in-between color, like a goat's eyes. The expression of the eyes didn't change although the old face puckered up into a slow, wry smile.

"That was close, partner. Darned close. You got it once in the back. That one plowed through the meat and come out on the point of your shoulder blade. Followed the bone until it come out. Other one went into your face under the jaw. Never even touched a bone, but it sure tore a hole in the hide, there. Don't know for sure, but I think the slug went out your mouth." The goat eyes were speculative. "You recollect whether your mouth was open or not, when you got it?"

In spite of his soreness, weakness and general dejection, Troy grinned slightly. He studied the old face for a second before he answered.

73

"Don't remember a thing. Nothing; until I woke up here."

"Yeah." The old man's disappointment was obvious. "Well—just wondered. Your bushwhackers sure like back targets. Both them shots was fired from behind you." The man's glance went casually over Troy's big outline under the quilts. He shrugged matter-of-factly. "Don't know as I blame 'em, though. If I was fixin' to cross a big buck like you, I'd take the best target too."

"How'd you find me, anyway?"

"Wasn't hard. You was riding a Roman-nosed bay horse I sold the liveryman over in Herd's Crossing. Every time the old cuss comes in this direction, he tries to bring his passenger to the cabin, here. He come in with blood all over the saddle. Fresh blood. I just back-tracked him and there you was." The man wagged his head ruefully.

"But—I'll tell you. Next time I hope it's a smaller feller. Had one devil of a time getting you across a horse to bring you back." There was a short lull, then, "Why'd they do it, partner?"

Troy looked into the face and saw a similarity in its weathered, tough exterior, and thought back to Cookie. He'd have to take the chance, though, on this oldtimer. Anyway, the old cuss had probably been into his wallet, so there wouldn't be much sense in being cagey. The old man listened stoically as Troy spoke, slowly, haltingly, and his hazel eyes reflected nothing that would give an inkling of the thoughts behind them, then, when Troy had finished, he swore softly.

"Nice friends you got. Well—I know your name because I seen in your purse. Sent word to Bannock about you, figuring you might die. You're pretty darned big to be digging a hole for in this hardpan." He chuckled. "But you'll make it, all right, now."

Troy nodded abstractly. "You—a friend of Jeb Carter's?"

"Nope. Don't even know the man except by hearsay." The hazel eyes winked gravely. "Don't worry, feller. I got reasons for living here, too. They're old reasons, but I learnt one thing from 'em, years back. How to keep my mouth shut. You got nothing to worry about from me."

"What's your name?"

"Gillespie. Lee Gillaspie. Your's is Troy Muller."

Troy was at Lee Gillaspie's place for almost two full weeks before he could feel the strength flow back into him in full tide, then he borrowed Lee's horse, carbine and saddle, and rode back. Left four-hundred in paper money that Lee could've stolen from him, and didn't, and went back over the same route he'd left Herd's Crossing by, only it was twilight now, with the promise of darkness in the sky before he reached the town.

There were sunken places in his face. The softness had vanished from around his middle and the suffering in his eyes had mated with rancor and produced an offspring of coldness, of calculating, shrewd deadliness that was like ice.

Herd's Crossing accepted him into its outskirts with indifference. Another grub-liner who preferred to leave his horse back in a scraggly clump of oaks at the far end of town.

The riders on the plankwalk ignored the massive man who swung in behind the cafe across from the liverybarn, and went gingerly around the refuse piles until he was at the rear door of the little building, knuckling softly for admittance.

He could hear the growing bedlam in a nearby saloon that reminded him of the Palace, while he waited. His face had a faint, unreal looking smile on it when the door opened a crack, enough to admit a big boot as a wedge, then Troy shouldered inside and saw the huge old pistol staring at him far below the withered mask of fear and horror that erupted on to Cookie's face.

"Put the gun away, Cookie, I didn't come here for revenge." The gun wavered but never lowered. Cookie's teeth were in. He flicked a leathery tongue over the lips and backed away stiffly. Oddly, too, Troy didn't feel any animosity against the man who had tipped off his mortal enemies.

"All right; if it makes you feel better, keep it. Listen, I want some information from you."

"You'll get—lead, that's all, boy; just lead."

Troy shook his head, seeing the fright heighten but not particularly afraid. "Cookie; I'll give you a hundred dollars cash for the answer to just one question."

"Nossir. Not on your damned life. He'd kill me."

"Maybe, but I doubt it. You see, I'm going to kill him. You've got darned little to worry about, there."

"Hah!" It rang with sarcasm. "You'll never get close enough. Jeb's a wily coyote."

"I know that, Cookie. We were in business together. But—don't sell me short, either. One-hundred in paper money."

The old horse pistol drooped a little, but not much, and not from indecision either; from sheer weight in the withered, tired old hand.

"Well—by damn; he didn't get you at that."

Troy's smile returned a little lopsidedly. "No, but no thanks to you because he didn't. Like I said—don't sell me short, either. He did his best, Cookie. It wasn't good enough though, was it? I'm still around."

"Yeah. That goshdarned one-eyed son of—"

"Just tell me where Jeb is."

"He didn't do it, boy."

"Sure not. He'd hire it done, now. Anyway, I don't care who those two hombres were. I want Jeb, not his flunkies. For a hundred-dollars and a tight trap, Cookie. You got my word on it. Nothing'll ever come out of me on this."

Another flick of the moist, dank old tongue over bloodless lips. "It'd be a gamble at that. Two to one're good odds."

"Two to one?"

The old head bobbed up and down, once. "Sure; he'll kill you, stranger. That'll seal your lips. If he don't and you kill him, he'll never know either. My odds. The other one is that neither of you kills the other—then you might talk."

"No danger there. I told you—"

"I'm not taking anybody's word. Haven't in fifty years and won't now."

"All right, don't. You want the hundred or do I shoot it out with you? I owe you a little something, Cookie. I know who passed the word on me."

The big old pistol came up swiftly but it didn't seem to have the same menace any more. "You dassen't, boy. I'd drop you'll in your tracks."

Troy shook his head slowly. "You might, but then again, you might not, and if you didn't, Cookie, you'd be the deadest cook Herd's Crossing has ever seen. Come on—don't be a horse's butt; take the hundred and rest easy." Troy was watching the old man's face. A lot of the fright had vanished and was replaced by avarice. A hundred dollars then, to a man like Cookie, was a fortune. He'd sold out worse men for much less, too, in his long life.

"Cookie; I haven't got all night. Take the hundred or pull that damned trigger."

Cookie's breathing was audible in the gloomy, reflected light of the small kitchen. He clenched tighter on the gun butt, then let it sag away when he nodded.

"Let's see the hundred."

After that it was easy. Troy watched him fondle the crumpled bills as he talked, tossing the old gun aside and forgetting it. "North out of town about ten miles you'll see what's left of a burnt out stage coach. There's a little saddleback trail takes off northeast from the wreck. Follow it plumb to the end and you'll be in the house yard of a man's ranch. Place's owned by Jeb. He keeps this old gaffer who used to own it, as a sort of hired man who runs things for him. Got a few legitimate cattle—and such."

Troy was wondering how he'd know when Cookie was lying. The last sentence sold him right off, because he, too, had been a dupe for Jeb Carter. He nodded and shoved off the wall, fished around in his pocket, found two twenties, and tossed them beside Cookie's pile.

"For not lyin', Cookie. Want some advice?"

"What?"

"Get t'hell out of Herd's Crossing and don't even look back. Jeb's no fool."

"If you keep your word, I got nothing to worry about."

"I'll keep it all right, but like I said—he's no damned fool. Remember, I doped you out, and he isn't nearly as dead as I was, when I guessed about you."

"Ain't worrying." Cookie's fingers kept toying with his fortune. His eyes had a glittering half-light that was

78

as evil as it was ugly. "Besides—one of you's goin' to die, and I win, no matter who loses." He lifted a long, thin upper lip. The contrast between the shining, perfectly even teeth and the ravaged old face they were set in, was a study in contrasts. Troy noticed, shrugged and went back out into the night. He had what he wanted and moved back along the alley route until he was to his horse. Swinging up he stared back at the Crossing and grunted to himself. It was even less attractive by night, than by day—if that was possible.

The burned old coach was lying on its side. The upper wheels had been taken off. There was little to show the thing had ever been a coach of any kind—or anything else, for that matter. Troy leaned far forward in the weak moonlight, saw the meandering little saddlehorse trail and rode over it.

The coolness had a chilling effect on him after the warmth of the cafe. His mind drifted off the purpose of the ride and went back to Bannock; to Ellie and Tom. He wondered if Tom lived and what Ellie thought, not having heard from him in over two weeks. He'd write her; still, after tonight there'd be no need to write. He intended to ride back anyway. He'd see her tomorrow—or never.

His face was sore where the bullet hole was a white splotch of scar-tissue under the jaw. He probed it gently, feeling the malleable stiffening of the scar's core, and let his hand drop away to his gun. He examined it carefully, returned it to the holster and rode over the still, forbidding land in its ancient blanket of semi-moonlighted blackness.

The trail absorbed a good hour and half's riding. It twisted conveniently to avoid clumps of trees and scattered wisps of sage and chaparral brush, until a switchback that twisted sharply over a small ridge, showed the tiny light-pricks of orange lantern light down ahead, in a half hidden swale, that meant a habitation. He reined up, looking down at it. He was close to the end of the trail—one way or the other.

A flock of irrelevant thoughts rushed in but he cleared his mind of them in a flash. Whatever the reason, the course and purpose that put him there on the ridge above Carter's hideout, wasn't important now. Just one thing mattered from here on. Whether he would live or not, and this depended on whether he killed his man—or not.

He went down across the cold land angling away from the place, testing the wind, which was negligible but strong enough to carry scent, and skirted the ranch. No dogs challenged his passing. Satisfied, Troy found some scrub oaks nestled in dark shadows and left his horse there, shed his spurs, took down Lee's ancient, hexagon-barreled old carbine, and went ahead slowly, hunting for cover, which was almost non-existent around the ranch, and studied the buildings as he went.

There was an ancient barn with a brand, spanking new roof, two sets of out-buildings, one of which was apparently an unoccupied bunkhouse that backed on to a blacksmith's shop, and a little apart, the main house. It had been whitewashed recently and stood out eerily in the ghostly moonlight.

There was a light at both ends of the main house, as though the main, darkened rooms between, were a sort of barrier between the actual owner's quarters, and the supposed owner's rooms.

Troy watched and became convinced. It all fitted into the pattern he had worked out in his mind about Jeb Carter. This was the place all right. He hadn't followed the trail into the yard, naturally, to find out whether it ended at this ranch or not, but he was confident anyway.

There was bound to be other men on the place as well as Jeb. He thought back to the two men who had shot him down. They might be in the dark bunkhouse. If not them, surely others. Jeb Carter was a lone wolf, he knew, but at his hideout he'd want company and there would always be lesser men to supply it.

Troy got almost to the bunkhouse by following the dark tracery of the barn's shadows, then he raised his step, clumped down heavily—not too heavily—on the stoop, lifted the latch and went into the jet blackness that smelled of human beings and horse sweat, with a low, deliberately muffled song on his lips. He was in the middle of the room before anyone challenged him.

The voice was disgruntled, thick and garrulous. "That you, Jeb? F'hell's sake shut up."

Troy located the man and the bunk. There were two men there. Opposite each other in lowers. One fast glance showed the rest of the bunks unoccupied. He raised his gun and arced it viciously, twice. One man leaped convulsively inside his smelly quilts when the blow struck, but the other man just sagged flatter under his coverlets and began to breathe in a ragged, tortured way.

It was minutes before he could see well enough in the blackness to locate the guns, but when he could, he took three pistols, four rifles and a brace of carbines still ensconced in sweat-stiff saddleboots, and went back outside, where the atmosphere was less polluted. A few seconds' walk put him beside a thick old trough full of green slime and sulfurous smelling water. The guns went in one at a time, silently, then he moved back into the shadows of the bunkhouse again and studied the

81

main house. Only the lights at the east end of the building still burned. He guessed this would be Jeb and started to shove out of the shadows to approach, when something billowy white and swiftly moving, almost floating, came around the back of the house and hurried toward the rear of the barn.

Startled, Troy watched until the ghostly apparition had vanished from his view behind the barn, then he turned swiftly, retraced his own steps down the log siding until he was close to the rear, lay down and shoved his head around a corner, chip deep in fetid dust. The white shadow was gone. He lay there frowning and thoughtful. Whoever it was—whatever it was—he couldn't have it roaming around behind him, which would be the case as soon as he crossed the yard and went to the house.

Slowly, he pushed himself erect and crouched. There was the blacksmith's shop behind the bunkhouse, and there was a neglected, tangled old grape arbor off to the west a little ways back from any building. Also, there was the opened maw of the old barn. The apparition might have entered any of the three. He watched for movement, swore when he saw none, or anything white either, then scrambled fast back around to the front of the barn, entered with his gun clutched and cocked in his fist, and went the full length of the place. The ghost hadn't entered the barn. Irritably, he peered from the rear opening and decided on the blacksmith's shop next. It could be reached without too much exposure.

The thunder of his own heart within its cavernous prison sounded unnaturally loud to him. He went over to the shop, tried the door and felt his palms get slippery with sweat when the thing threatened to squeak. It was a long ten minutes of nerve racking labor before he had an opening sufficiently wide to allow him to peer into the gloomily old place, redolent of coke and cooling steel, from behind the door. Empty. There wasn't a soul inside. He pulled back wide eyed, speculating on a way to approach the old arbor, which was set apart and with open clearings of bare land on all sides.

There was only one way to do it. Frontally, openly and lazily, as though he neither expected to meet anyone there or expected not to. Still, the tag ends of his nerves were rubbed raw and quivering from the prolonged tension. Too, he knew the men in the bunkhouse wouldn't stay unconscious indefinitely. He had intended to rush the house, find Jeb and shoot it out with him, when he'd clubbed the sleeping men. For that purpose, his savage pistol blows had been sufficient. Now, however, he reckoned he'd spent a good fifteen minutes trying to find the illusive ghost that had disappeared somewhere in the yard.

Pushing himself into plain view and walking as though he had come from the bunkhouse, his hand bent and hanging above the sweat stained old walnut of Tom Buffum's .45, Troy went forward slowly, leisurely, watching the grape arbor with eyes slitted and unblinking; owlish, intent eyes.

But there was no burst of gunfire. Not even any swearing in astonishment by a startled outlaw, when he turned abruptly and entered the tangled mass of fragrant, rank old vines, and saw the figure ahead of him, erect and waiting.

It was a woman and she stood in his path, leaning forward a little and trying to see into his face, made dark by the shadows of the place, and darker by some errant clouds over the sickly moon the moment he entered the arbor. She may not have recognized Troy, but he knew who she was the instant he was close. He stopped in shock, his breath coming out past parted lips as though under extreme pressure. It was just exactly the second he stopped, stock still and motionless, that the vagrant wisps of cloud banners shifted, and the pallor of a quartered moon showed him plainly. Then she knew him instantly.

A hand went up over her mouth. She bit the back of it with small teeth. Her large eyes went wide and awry. Frantic, frightened and horrified, all at once. Then, to Troy's astonishment, she collapsed at his feet

There was a long moment of indecision, then he bent, scooped her up, looked around and struck out for the barn where he had recalled seeing a water trough. Inside, it was like the bottom of a well. He found a small, loose shock of hay, eased her down on it, got a hatful of water and threw it in her face.

The elemenl of surprise was his, so far. If he lost that, he'd probably lose his life as well. Cin's appearance had jolted him badly, but he still clung to the need for secrecy at Carter's hideout, and meant to have it. Cin or no Cin!

CHAPTER SIX

CIN'S FACE WAS HEIGHTENED IN ITS BEAUTY BY THE soft light that filtered into the old barn. She stared up at him through the sheen of water that dripped from her, making no move to ackowledge the wetness at all. The shock was still in her eyes but the paralysis was gone.

"Troy—you're—you're—"

"Alive," he finished for her. "Yeah. Alive and loaded

for bear, Cin. Where's Jeb?"

She continued to stare at him, then, after a moment she shuddered. "That—was awful. Like seeing a— ghost. God!"

"Rope it; where's Jeb?"

"I—don't know. What are you going to do to me?"

He considered this for a second, then shrugged. "That depends on you. Among men, you'd be killed. Jeb told me how you've been trying to hire someone to kill me. It wouldn't surprise me a damned bit to find out you sent those two gunmen to drygulch me."

"No—Troy. That was Jeb. He—heard about you being in Herd's Crossing from an old man down there who's his watcher. I—didn't know—exactly—until later."

"Cin, you're a liar. You're worse than a liar. How do you like living with Jeb?" He tossed his head irritably. "You've always thought I was a fool. Like the night you told me you weren't ashamed that you knew Jeb— danced with him. That's telling me you thought what he did was all right. Sure Cin, I'm dumb. I reckon—must be or I wouldn't be in this fix now—but I'm not that doggoned dumb. But I'm not going to take revenge for you living with the lousiest outlaw in the country and using my name while you're doing it." He hesitated, seeing the bewilderment crowd into her face.

"What—then, Troy?"

"I'm going to hit you like you wanted to hit me. Where it'll really hurt. I'm going to kill the man you've taken up with. He'll be dead, but you'll go on living, and every day of your life you'll remember what you lost, and I hope to God it drives you crazy, thinking of the husband you've lost—and the free spending lover; Jeb Carter."

85

She was white faced but not too badly shaken in spite of the earnestness in his words, and for good reason, too. She made a grimace of a smile and shook her head slowly at him. "No you won't, Troy. You damned fool, you're no match for Jeb Carter and never were. He'll kill you like a sick dog. You'll see."

Her confidence irritated him a lot more than Cookie's had, but he thought of what he'd told the cafe owner.

It gave him a measure of confidence again.

"Maybe, Cin. You might be right, but remember Jeb sent out two gunmen to do that job before—and I'm still around. Sure; I understand why you want to sell me short, but don't be too confident."

The doubt was there, suddenly, and with it a sort of restrained panic. She blinked her eyes at him and pressed her palms together over his stomach, then her glance fell and saw the worn old carbine, the tied down gun and the leaner, harder look to him. The gray eyes swept back up to his face and lingered there, reading the bitterness, coldness and craftiness that had become a part of his features lately. The doubt grew within her more than ever. This wasn't Troy Muller the hulking blacksmith, nor Troy Muller the wealthy owner of the Palace Bar either. It was a new man, one she'd never seen or known before, fired with something hidden and volatile and determined. Even his unshaven, rough appearance in the faded clothes, and skin berry brown from sunblast, made him foreign to her. Fear mixed in with the doubt, then.

"Troy—what's—changed you? Listen; I'll go away. I'll take—"

"You can go to the devil, Cin. You're headed that way anyway. What's changed me? A lot of things. You're one of 'em. Jeb's another. Thinking has helped too, Cin. Then—Jeb shot down Tom Buffum. I've made a long list of mistakes and I'm out to square 'em."

"And—Ellie? What about her?"

"I'm going to marry her, Cin, as soon as I shed you." He thought of Tom and his heart sank. He and Ellie would never marry if Tom was dead. It was as certain as falling leaves in autumn. Hoarsely he added, "If I can."

"If you can shed me?" Cin misunderstood. "You can. I've already started divorce proceedings, here at the Crossing."

His smile was sardonic. "Well—I'm glad to hear that. Only I can't wait."

"What do you mean?"

"I'd rather be a widower!"

Horror spread like a mottled blanket over her face. "Troy! God Almighty, Troy!"

He saw the way her shoulders hunched spasmodically. Normally he'd have felt compassion, now he didn't. "Well—you were willing to be a widow, weren't you?"

"No I swear—"

"Don't bother. More lies. How about Jennings? You didn't send him to Bannock to kill me? You didn't tell Jeb to either, I don't suppose. Only difference is, Jeb offered to hogtie you and bring you back to me, when he was through with you."

"I told Jennings about you. He was crazy mad. Troy; he was young, excitable—"

"And now he's dead. All right; to the devil with him. What about the two gunmen who rode me down? You didn't know about them, did you?"

"I swear I didn't, Troy. Not until later. Jeb told me after they'd come back."

"And Jeb?"

"Jeb—he said he wouldn't do it as long as you ran the Palace for him. Then—after you fought him—he changed."

"I reckon," Troy said drily. "So—you think everyone else should die—but not you. Cin, I've got less feeling about you than a snake; a goddamned snake."

"Troy!" She was petrified with fear. The last vestiges of fury and doubt were gone. He looked lethal to her—and was. She knew it, too.

"Where's Jeb?"

"He—left just before I came out, tonight."

"You're lying, Cin."

"No. I swear I'm not."

"What were you doing out there, in that old grape arbor?"

"I—there's a rider here—on the ranch. Young fellow. I—"

"Oh! Another one. You were going to send him after me like you did that fool Jennings. That it?"

"Don't make—"

Troy's words were soaked in scorn. "Forget it. I'm not interested. Where did Jeb go?"

"Please—I don't know."

His patience was tattered. One quick step forward and he had one big paw over her mouth to stifle the screams that were rising in panic into her throat.

He held her like that until the gray eyes closed and a terrible quaking took over and dissipated itself, then he let her go.

"Give me the truth, Cin—and right now!"

"He—we—talked it over. He—said we needed more money."

"Where is he? Cut out the rest of it."

"He went to Bannock—to rob the bullion stage out at

88

dawn."

The surprise in Troy's eyes was abrupt and stunning. Tom was flat on his back. The stage belonged to the Keystone Line and he owned half of that company. Campbell had said they'd lose the franchise if they were held up once more. Gripping Cin's arm, hard, he shook her gently.

"How long ago did he ride out?"

"Just before—I came out here. An hour, Troy?"

He didn't answer. There was nothing here to hold him any longer. Jeb was riding toward Bannock, so leaving Cin behind at the ranch wouldn't make much difference. She couldn't rouse the knocked-out renegades in the bunkhouse in time to stop him, and he had no intention of ever returning here anyway. He had one job to do. He'd either do it, or fail. Either way he'd never return. Focusing his dark eyes on Cin's face again, he nodded at her. "All right, Cin. You saddle up a horse and ride. Keep on riding. Don't stop until you're so far from Bannock and Herd's Crossing folks won't ever have heard of 'em. You understand me?"

"Yes. I'll—do it. Now—tonight."

He turned away, studying the stalled horses, saw one he liked and went forward to halter it, letting the rest of what he had to say slide back over one shoulder to her.

"Better take your kid cowboy with you, too. You might need another damned fool to sacrifice, before you're too old to interest men."

He didn't see the resurgence of wild hatred that came into her level eyes, along with his reprieve to her. He didn't even suspect it until he had led the breedy, fast looking horse out to where his own animal was tied, swung up into the saddle and started off in a long lope, leading the spare horse. The only way he knew definitely that Cin's murderous zeal wasn't abated an iota in spite of her bad moments before, when she had feared him so much, was when the orange stab of flame leaped out of a clump of brush on his route of travel, a few hundred feet from the ranch buildings. And even then, he wasn't sure. The men in the bunkhouse, maybe, had revived, although he doubted it, or there may have been another man somewhere on the ranch. In the main house for instance, but he didn't believe it at all.

That would be Cin. He grunted and bent low, knowing the shadows were his allies now, and didn't even bother to reach for his own gun or return the fire. Not even after a second, then a third, shot, probed the night, searching for him, using the dull thunder of his horse's hooves in passing, as a loose, generalized target. There wasn't any particular danger to him and he knew it. Luck might interfere—or destiny—but marksmanship in the dark against an unseen, rapidly moving target, would never bring him down.

He rode fast and let the cold air force tears out the corners of his eyes in spite of his squint. With an hour's start Jeb would be far ahead, still, the outlaw wouldn't be riding hard for two reasons. One, he had the entire night before him and didn't have to make his stand before sun-up, and two, he'd want to conserve his horse's strength. Moreover, only two people knew Carter's life was in danger. Troy and Cin. He smiled coldly into the night. Cin's hatred wouldn't overwhelm her sense. She'd never give him another chance to get close to her; not after shooting at him, which was the same as telling him she'd never honor her promises to leave the country, or quit planning to have him killed.

The land rocketed by in silhouette. Dimensions were obscured until everything looked flat and dark, without depth or solidness There were no grays, no shades of night at all. Just black and blacker. Near objects assumed perspective, shape and familiarity, then were lost behind in the rhythmic movement of the horse he rode. He watched the landmarks come up reluctantly in the near distance, in the limited scope of his vision, stand for a few seconds before him, then whip away to the rear. Each symbol of the miles behind made him feel excitement, then Gillaspie's horse began to stumble and run in a mechanical, blind way.

Troy changed horses about eleven miles from Bannock. Gillaspie's horse watched him lope off and followed shufflingly, still eager but lacking the stamina to keep up the pace. The new horse—the one he'd taken from Carter's ranch—was much smoother in his gait and more powerful of limb and wind. There were great stores of unused energy still inside the animal when Troy reined him to a walk and held him there in spite of his head tossing and cake-walking.

Bannock wasn't far ahead through the darkness. He couldn't see it but he knew this end of the country like the back of his hand. Somewhere ahead was Jeb Carter. The outlaw would have a place in mind to ambush the stage. It troubled Troy, too, because he was only one man and there were dozens of spots ideal for holding up the coach.

He reined up suddenly and considered his own disadvantages. They were almost limitless. If Carter fired his gun when he stopped the stage, Troy would hear, be able to gauge the direction of the sound and head for it. However, if Jeb didn't use his gun, which was more than likely, Troy wouldn't even know where to look.

He sat slumped over, scowling into the gloom. There

seemed to be, almost, some providence protecting Jeb Carter. Keeping Troy from finding him; killing him.

The sky was still black along the flat, uneven edges of the world. He was staring at its vague outlines when the idea came to him. There were only two ways he could find Jeb. One would be to follow the stage, and the other would be to be on it. The latter, for multiple reasons instantly apparent, appealed the most to him. He looked anxiously at the horizon again, guessed he could make Bannock by hard, devious riding, and struck out.

It would be close. Having no watch, he could only surmise the hour, still, the night had an icy feeling of near dawn, and that meant the hostlers would be working over the coach and harnessing the teams right now.

He let the breedy, big horse plummet through the darkness recklessly, belly down and ears back, covering great gobs of ground with each stride. And he cursed savagely at the necessity that made him avoid the roadway and it's near country, for fear the outlaw would hear his horse racing through the night, or, worse yet, see him riding toward Bannock.

He thought of his closeness to Ellie, and instantly the bitter-sweet memories swept over him. The wistfulness too, because he really doubted if Tom still lived. In order to stifle the agony of suspense, of knowing he would be within walking distance of finding out, actually, when he roared up beside the stage, and still not be able to spare time to find out, he switched his mind to the stage line itself.

Loring Campbell, for all his softness and quiet voice, had never been a man Troy liked. That they were partners meant nothing to Troy. He'd known Campbell ever since he had come to Bannock and started up the

Keystone Line. The man was ruthless, cold, and as wily as an old fox. There was something deadly about the man's fishy, perpetually watering eyes. Not courageously deadly, but strategically deadly. Troy shrugged to himself. He owned half interest in the line and, up to now, Campbell had run the thing. That way, they hit it off well enough, but Troy's scorn for Loring Campbell was still there, inside of him.

Suddenly there was a jumble of lighter outlines against the somber hues of the night. He smiled in uneasy triumph. It was Bannock again, as squatly and dreary looking as ever—but it was also home, a place he hadn't really expected to see again. Not after he'd met the gunhawks who rode him down, and again, when he rode into Carter's ranch determined to kill the outlaw.

The breedy big horse was leaking air now, like a gas jet. Troy pulled him back into a slow lope, then gradually, with the lessening sounds of the animal's breathing, eased him into a kidney rattling trot and finally a long legged walk as he entered the north end of town and fought down his own desire to hurry.

There were lanterns burning softly from within the coach shed and horse-barn adjoining the Keystone Line's cramped little office. He let a great sigh out and reached up to dab at the clammy perspiration above his mouth.

Men were working in silence. Some loading bullion boxes of heavy oak with forged hinges and locked hasps, inside the chartered coach. Others were fumbling with horse harness with hands stiff from lack of sleep and cold. He swung down outside, looped the reins around a hitchrail and walked toward the doorway of the place. A man materialized out of the shadows beside the door. Reflected light glinted on a studdy, menacing shotgun he held.

"What you want, stranger?"

Troy grunted his surprise, then recalled that this was no usual scheduled stage. He smiled at the shotgun guard. "I'm Troy Muller. Own half this stage line. Loring Campbell around?"

If he'd said he was the Devil himself, the man's face couldn't have shown more astonishment. The riot gun came up and pointed directly at Troy's belt buckle. There was a loud, explosive curse from somewhere inside the shed. Troy's smile faded in bewilderment.

"What ails you, man?"

The guard's voice came back slowly, very, very softly. "You," he said. "You're—wanted, Troy. What in hell'd you have to come back here for?"

Dumbfounded, the big man gasped, read the obvious truth in the guard's eyes, and stood motionless. "Wanted? For what?"

"For a passel of things, according to Campbell. For planning the robberies of these bullion stages that've happened up to now, for one thing. For instigating the shooting down of Sheriff Buffum, for another." The shotgun shifted a little. "For a passel of things."

"Loring Campbell—started all this, partner?"

The man shrugged. "He—didn't do nothing to stop it."

"But—what right's he got—?" The futility of talking bore in on Troy. Gradually, just one thing became uppermost in his mind. He had to get away. To get clear of this riot gun that held him rigid, as surely as though he were hobbled. He had to do it fast, too, before someone sauntered out of the shed and saw him. Set up the cry. He swallowed hard, fighting off the black despair that was settling over him in waves.

"Listen; you the riding guard?"

The man nodded. "Yeah. I'm riding shotgun and Lew Carver's driver. Why?"

"What's your name?"

"Don't make no difference—Troy—but it's Birch Hardin."

Troy remembered the man vaguely as a silent, soft spoken patron of the Palace. He knew none of Campbell's hirelings anyway.

"All right Birch. I'm in a spot."

"I'll say you are." It was almost humorously dry, the way he said it, but the shotgun didn't waver.

"No, not the way you think. I don't understand Campbell's idea in raking me at all, but it's beside the point. The thing is, I've ridden two horses damned near to death to get here before the bullion coach went out. Jeb Carter's out on the north road somewhere, fixing to hold it up."

The guard's eyes were wide and fixed. "How'd you find this out?"

Troy made a gesture of annoyance with one big arm. "That doesn't matter either. All that matters is that you've got to be prepared."

"Where'll it happen?"

"Damned if I know. I rode here hoping to find Carter. One man can't do it, so I rode on it to get on the stage and go along, this trip."

"Then we'd have one inside and one outside, wouldn't we?"

Troy understood readily enough. He looked at the man closely. "Birch—if you think I'm a killer and the rest, why'n hell are you standing there talking to me? Why don't you yell out?"

The guard grunted sofly. "Well; t'tell the truth, I don't believe that stuff Campbell's been handing out.

95

Most folks do, though. I'm just standing here puzzling out what to do."

"How can I get on that stage."

"You can't. That's out"

"I've got to, darn it. Carter's got the advantage of you and the driver and you know it. You two'll be up on the box. He'll jump when he's good and ready. Knowing he's going to, isn't going to help you much. You're sitting ducks for a man on the ground, behind a rock maybe, up on that box."

"And—what can you do about it?"

"I'll be inside. Everyone knows the bullion coaches don't carry passengers. All I want is one shot at him."

The guard recalled some gossip he'd heard around town. That Troy Muller's wife had run off with the outlaw. It gave weight to Troy's plan for a shot at the renegade. The shotgun muzzle drooped a little and a long, cold silence settled between the men, then the guard spoke with a short nod.

"I'm a damned fool to do this, Troy. If just half of what Campbell says is true, I'm putting an outlaw inside the coach, and behind Lew and me, as well as knowing there's to be one out front too." He shrugged. "But— we're sitting ducks anyway, I reckon, and the run's scheduled so's we don't dare hold it up longer'n sun-up." The shotgun drooped all the way and was eased off-cock. "What a darned mess."

"How'll I get in the coach?"

The guard leaned back against the building, regarding Troy through shrewd, thoughtful eyes. "That's no problem. I'm in charge of the night crew. You just stay out here in the dark until Lew wheels out. He'll stop while I climb up. You use this near side door and get in. But watch out; don't let any of the hostlers see you."

Troy nodded and shrugged. "That won't make much difference, Birch. Once we're rolling, nothing'll count but meeting Jeb Carter. After that—well—everyone can know I'm aboard."

"All right, but listen. You're an outlaw around Bannock. If the worst happens, I'm relying on you never to say I even saw you before you climbed into the coach. Your word?"

"My word."

The guard nodded his head slowly, then pushed off the building. "You'd better get over here in the shadows. I'll take a look and see how the boys're making out then be back."

Troy faded easily into a narrow crevice between the stage line office and the mercantile store beside it. He tasted the antagonism he'd always felt toward Loring Campbell, in his mouth. The man had done an obvious thing. He'd known how Bannock's sentiments, from gossip, had estranged him to the townsmen. His prolonged absence had been a wonderful opportunity for placing his silent partner forever beyond the pale of respectability, and thus Campbell would retain control of his stage line—and Troy's money—as well.

Resentment boiled inside of him. He was still seething when Birch Hardin strolled over with elaborately casual steps, and nodded up into his face.

"Be about ten minutes yet, Troy. I been thinking—"

"Sure, and you've got doubts. I can't do any more'n tell you I swear to what I'm saying. Carter's out for the bullion shipment. Don't ask me how he knows it's going out. He just does."

"Yeah, I reckon. Lew might not like this." The man's deepset eyes saw bewilderment on Troy's face. "Lew— the driver."

"Oh. Yeah; well, after we're rolling, you tell him. I'll watch for reaction. If it gets mad, I'll take his gun—but I hope that isn't necessary, because we may need it before the night's over."

"You reckon Carter'll have help?"

"No, I don't think so. Jeb usually works alone. We won't know though, until he stands up and calls us out."

"No," Birch said softly. He looked closer at Troy. "I'm probably the biggest horse's butt in Bannock—right now."

Troy recognized the man's remorse and doubt, but there wasn't anything he could truthfully add to what he'd already said. "Tell me something, Birch. Did—Tom Buffum—die?"

The night seemed to pull back into itself while he waited for the answer. Even the noises of the hostlers at work over the coach inside the shed, behind them, seemed to cease for a bare fraction of a second. Troy's world was teetering precariously and his heart was pounding a slow, somber dirge in his ears.

Birch looked at him in surprise. "You have been out of things for a while, haven't you?"

Troy didn't even nod. He stood in stiff silence, waiting; hoping with every fiber of his being. Then the guard shoved his cold hands down inside his pants pocket and shook his head.

"No. It was close though. For about a week the doc wouldn't say one way or the other. He's pretty chipper now, though, Tom is." The faded eyes swung back to Troy's face. "That's the main reason I never yelled out or pulled the triggers when you came up, Troy. I never knew you well, but Tom and I always have been friends. He told you had made mistakes all right, but that you didn't have nothing to do with his shooting. Said he'd deputized you to catch Carter, too." Birch shook his head again, looking down at his booted feet. "But—well—a man never knows, for sure, does he? I mean—Bannock's full of talk. Most of it's against you."

Troy didn't answer. There was nothing to say anyway. The guard had summed it up pretty well, pro and con. A man never knows, for sure. He thought of Ellie and tried to find a prayer of thankfulness. For the second time that he could remember, the vacuum in that direction, the complete lack of knowing any prayer at all, any kind, was borne in upon him. He recalled how he'd strived to find something appropriate in his memory the night Tom was shot. This time it annoyed him, the void, so glaring and embarrassing, where some way of tendering gratitude to some vaguely Almighty Being, should have been. It made his sense of loneliness come up out of nowhere, suddenly. Made him abruptly aware that this same loneliness was based, factually, on this very shortcoming.

He was turning it over in his mind and finding pleasure in the discovery, too, even as he made up a rough, humble little prayer of his own, and offered it up for the chance that existed anew for him and Ellie.

Then a man came to the lighted doorway of the shed and growled garrulously at the guard. "She's ready, Birch. Lew's coming."

The protesting sound of great weight moving sluggishly on well greased axles emerged from the doorway. Already, some of the hostlers, their chore done for the time being, were blowing down the lamp mantles and making desultory talk, hardly glancing at the big coach and its plump, powerful horses.

When the swaying, scarred vehicle emerged into the night, Birch Hardin was deliberately on the far side. The

99

driver pulled up on his lines, leaned far over and watched the guard clamber up.

On Troy's side there was only the deep blackness and purple interior of the stage. He was inside almost before the vehicle had stopped for the guard. A sharp, angling corner of a bullion box gouged his shin cruelly. He swore under his breath and looked at the heavy load of silver, arranged carefully to maintain equilibrium inside the coach.

The stage picked up speed gradually. Troy knew the driver was an experienced man. He didn't ease off on the lines until the animals had walked a good half a mile and were loosened up, then slowly, he brought them through their gaits until the old coach was rocking along gently and evenly, behind the mile eating gallop of the pullers.

CHAPTER SEVEN

THE SMOOTH MOTION OF THE COACH HAD A LULLING effect on its passenger. He wasn't sleepy particularly, but the constant little rocking made his spirit and body relax a little.

Hunger, more than any other physical discomfort, except the cold, nagged him. He recalled Lee Gillaspie's greasy meals with rueful longing, then he heard the men on the box, overhead, talking. He was leaning forward to poke his head out the driver's side of the coach when he felt the slightest change in the tempo of the horse's gait and knew the driver had clutched suddenly at his lines.

The words were mostly indistinct, but enough came down to Troy for him to understand. The driver was furious. His curses rattled shrilly from the high seat he shared with the shotgun guard. Troy leaned farther out, grasped an edging of wood and steadied himself. By arduous craning and twisting, he could see the man's profile. The jaw, lean and pointed, was corded over with bunched up muscles. The man's head was averted, partially, facing toward Birch Hardin, but Troy could feel the tension in him. It puzzled him, too. He had felt certain the driver would help him catch Jeb Carter.

One final glance at the man's face showed that nothing of the sort would happen. Reluctantly, he was reaching for the near holster, when Lew's fist slashed downward in unison with a furious oath directed at Birch. Their hands met over the pistol butt and the driver jerked his head around in astonishment and stared into Troy's upturned face. Quick as a flash, the hand sucked balled up and smashed downward. Troy couldn't protect himself except by averting his face and absorbing the blow on top of his head, which he did, even as he grabbed wildly at the driver's near leg and pulled with all the strength of his powerful shoulders.

They struck the ground together, both clawing at holsters jarred empty by their landing impact, then the driver was on his feet, lashing out furiously as Troy got up. A stab of pain went through the big man's shoulder. He back pedaled quickly, warding off the raining blows with one arm and sensing that his wounded shoulder, not fully recovered from the bushwhacker's bullet, had been wrenched and injured in the fall.

A savage strike glanced off his cheekbone and an oily warmth told him his skin had been broken. Fully recovered in balance and thoroughly angry now, Troy fought one armed, boring into the driver, who was nearly a height with him, with mad fury, beating down the man's wild onslaught of blows and blasting out once, twice, and a third time, and feeling the shocking jar each time he met solid flesh.

Lew was staggering from a violent blow that slammed into his chest over the heart. He was head down and half sick, when Troy used his injured arm to shove him still farther back, then fired a looping, overhand blow that crumpled the leaner man instantly.

He turned, sucking air into his lungs that felt like hot tar, and looked for the stage. It had been stopped a short way off, turned wide off the road and was coming back toward them, horses at a walk. He waited until the vehicle was beside him, Birch Hardin, on the high seat, looping the lines around the set brake handle, staring down with an ugly look on his face, then Troy looked back quickly at the prostrate driver. A strange and sudden thought had occurred to him. Why had Carver been so vehement? So violently opposed to cooperating in the attempt to apprehend Jeb Carter?

He knelt down when Birch was beside him, rolled the unconscious driver over and slapped his face open handed, twice, sharply.

Birch growled and reached out to stop the blows. "Here, there's no call for that."

Troy watched Lew's eyes flicker and spoke without looking up at the guard. "Birch—why would he be so damned set against catching Carter?"

"I don't think it was that so much, as having you aboard. He just about exploded when I told him."

"That's what I mean. There's no reason for him to get so riled. Not like he did, anyway."

"You driving at something?"

Troy didn't answer. He was watching the driver regain consciousness slowly, push himself up and wag his head back and forth for a moment before he glanced

102

up at them, let his gaze drop from Birch to Troy and stay there, mirroring the worst kind of hatred.

Troy retrieved his gun, holstered it and stood lost in thought for a moment before he nodded and spoke. "Get up," he said.

The driver didn't move. Troy reached down and yanked him to his feet, steadied him for a second, then stepped back and frowned at him.

"Where's Jeb?"

"You—goshdarned fool! What the devil—are you talking about?"

"About how Jeb knew this was a bullion stage going out this morning. About where he's hiding on the trail—and all."

"You're crazy!"

Birch Hardin's face was creased into a mask of wonder. He was so absorbed with his thoughts that he made no move to stop the blow Troy fired at the driver, and he didn't step between them until Carver was on his knees again, then he faced Troy without resentment, this time, and showed his puzzlement.

"What you driving at, Troy. You think, because Jeb knows this is a bullion stage, someone told him?"

"How else would he know, Birch?" Troy nodded at the wobbly driver, getting slowly to his feet. "Someone told him—had to. My guess is that it would be someone like Lew here. Someone who'd know definitely when a bullion stage was going out. Jeb's got watchers. I know for a fact he has. Well; why else did Carver throw a fit when he knew what you and I were up to?"

Hardin turned slowly and stared at the groggy driver. His face showed amazement instead of wrath. "Lew— you did this? Passed the word to Carter—about the bullion?"

103

Carver glared at them both, ran a hand itchingly over the empty holster at his hip, and stood wide legged in indecision. He was a hard man, but when Troy started forward with an oath, he jerked his head sideways and spat bloody saliva before he spoke.

"All right. Yas. I passed the word. Jeb always checks with me when he's in Bannock."

"And," Troy asked. "Those other two bullion robberies on the line. You told him those schedules too?"

"Yas."

"What's your split, Lew?"

"A third."

Troy looked at Birch, saw the contempt and anger, and shrugged. "Get me some rope off the coach, will you, Birch?"

It didn't take long. The renegade driver was trussed up and thrown callously into the coach where the bullion boxes he had planned to divide with his outlaw friend, gouged into his flesh unmercifully.

Birch stood thoughtfully against the front wheel looking up at Troy. "Well; that messes everything up."

"How do you mean?"

The guard shrugged. "You'll have to drive now. Can't just one of us be up on the box or Carter'll suspect something."

Troy shrugged. "All right. What difference does it make it?"

"Not much," the guard said ironically, turning to climb up. "Just that now I got no one to back me up from down below. You'll be a sitting duck, too, up there. The surprise angle is shot to hades."

Troy climbed to the boot and shoved himself higher, on to the seat, and began to unloop the lines. "Can't be

104

helped, Birch. We've still got a little surprise left. At least Carter won't know until he stops us, that we're sort of expecting him."

The guard growled deep in his throat and threw Troy a saturnine look that said, as plainly as day, that this was indeed small compensation for being shot at by a topnotch gunslinger.

The horses edged back around on to the road, slack tugged on one side and tight tugged on the other, then the coach steadied itself behind the even tension and lurched forward, gathering speed gently again.

Troy didn't want them to be too far behind schedule, for fear Jeb Carter would become uneasy. He turned to Hardin when the horses were rocketing along easily in a mile eating lope that made their leather accouterments jingle rhythmically.

"You been driving long for Keystone?"

"Not driving. Shotgun guard. Yeah; about two years now."

"Ever been in one of their holdups?"

"On this run, to the Crossing, yeah. Twice. Both was bullion shipments, too. That's what startled me so bad back there. Lew was the driver both times. Now I look back, I can see things—little things—that make me sort of wonder, kind of."

Troy nodded. He was taking a liking to Birch Hardin. "You like guarding, Birch?"

"Used to. A man gets tired of getting up at three o'clock in the mornings, after he gets my age. Anyway, the Bannock end of things got no room for getting ahead. I been thinking about quitting." He threw a half-smile at Troy. "After tonight, finding out the driver I been partnering with these last couple of years is in with a darned outlaw, I got a better'n ever idea to chuck it."

Troy nodded. "You like the Herd's Crossing end of the line?"

"Well, a whale of a lot better'n this end."

"I'll make you an offer then. Keystone needs a new manager over there. You want the job?"

Hardin's head swiveled jerkily. He said nothing for a few hundred feet, then he chuckled. "Well—I'll take it providing you promise not to shoot me down. They say you're hard as hell on the Crossing's managers."

The sly reference to Will Jennings was expected, in a way. Troy smiled through his chagrin and nodded. "All right. You got my word on it."

"Then I'm Keystone's new manager at Herd's Crossing—that is—if Campbell don't cut a buck over it."

"He won't," Troy said quietly. Birch heard the undertone and shot him another quick look. He seemed on the verge of saying something, then apparently thought better of it because he shrugged slightly and swung his head back, letting the calm, faded eyes in his face roam carefully over the landscape ahead.

Troy pulled back when he figured they had made up their lost time, and let the horses jog easily through the cold predawn.

"You know Campbell pretty well, Birch?"

"Not very well. Just work for him. Fact is, I never cared overmuch for the man. Nothing in particular, just a lot of little things, sort of. A job's a job, though, and he darned seldom comes around giving orders, so I just sort of keep to myself. That's about the way thing's have been ever since I've ridden with Keystone. Why?"

"Well; I'm like you. Never cared for him. Not even when I bought into this line. It was a sound investment, I figured, so I took half interest."

"Well—where's that leave you?"

"Out on a limb, from the looks of things. Tell me—was Campbell appointed sheriff, or did he just sort of take it over by himself, while Tom is down?"

"Well, nearly as I heard, Tom deputized him from his sick bed."

"Yeah. Reckon he would at that. Tom figures Campbell's a friend of mine. He must think that, or I can't imagine him deputizing the man."

"Well," the guard said drily. "If he's a friend of your's, I hope I never have such a good friend."

Troy smiled widely. He found his respect and liking for this shotgun guard with the faded eyes and stubborn jaw, growing with each passing moment.

Birch turned to look at Troy. "Maybe Tom figures Campbell's a friend of your's because he's partner to you in the stage line. You reckon that might be it?"

"More'n likely."

"Well, whatever it is, I'm satisfied you're no running mate with Carver. Not after the way you figured Lew out, and took over from him."

There was a twinkle in Troy's dark glance, sidelong and appraising. "But, before that, you still had doubts?"

Birch shrugged. "Like I said back in Bannock. A man never knows, for sure."

"You took a long chance, then, if you felt that way."

"Not too long. I thought of a lot of things I've heard and seen. They didn't fit you or what Tom's told me about you. Anyway, we were scheduled and nobody, not even Jeb Carter, could turn us back." He shrugged. "I had to make a choice, and I made it," his face lighted up wryly. "Then I prayed I was doing the right thing."

"Never was any good at praying, myself," Troy said slowly, thoughtfully.

"No? Well—it's not too late to learn. Maybe it isn't anyway. See those rocks up ahead, off to your left there?"

Troy squinted at the pile of boulders tumbled against one another by some prehistoric joust of nature, and nodded. "Yeah. You reckon he'll be there?"

"Don't know, but that was the place Lew and I first got stopped. Close to two years ago. If I was you, I'd cock that gun and lay it in my lap."

Troy adopted the suggestion and forgot the biting cold as he switched the lines to his left hand and fondled the six-gun in his lap with a sweaty, clammy fist. He felt as conspicuous as a cowboy in church, sitting up there, exposed and bulking large over the top of the coach. It made him nervous, too, knowing that Birch, if he had to shoot, would lay the gun over in front of him, because the rocks were to the west of the road, on his side.

The ordeal was pure torture for both of them. The horses had never seemed to trot so slowly and the darkness appeared to have deepened by infinite shades all along the route of travel until they were approaching the boulders. Troy's eyes, still with cold, ached from the effort to see into the gloom, then they were abreast of the rocks, moving easily along, and finally past them, leaving them behind slowly but certainly.

Birch was relaxing against the seat again. Troy could feel the boards give. He breathed inward and out, twice, deeply, then turned to the guard.

"How far to the next likely place, Birch?"

"Well, if he uses the other spot where we was held up last year, it'll be about five miles from those rocks."

Troy nodded. "It'll take me that long to get my heart back down where it belongs."

Birch nodded without looking around. "Yeah; you

and me both."

The road wound uphill slightly. It wasn't a hard grade for the horses, but it was a gradual incline that tended to slow their progress Troy turned to his companion. "You reckon we're about on schedule? I'd hate to miss him."

Birch snorted. "You would? Not me, nossir; I wouldn't. Not when we're up on this darned seat like targets nailed to a tree." He spat lustily over the side, leaned far down, holding himself by one sinewy hand, and craned inside the coach It took considerable effort to regain the seat, but he turned to Troy with a nod.

"He's still in there. Don't look comfortable, though."

"I'm sure sorry for him." The sarcasm came readily. "How about the schedule?"

Birch nodded. "Close enough. I figure we made up lost time when you fogged it for a couple miles after the squabble. Anyway, these bullion coaches usually give or take a half an hour. Don't have to be so careful of contacting the Herd's Crossing station because they can't go anywhere until we get there. Not like hauling passengers."

Troy handed Birch the lines and rolled a cigarette. The match lighted up his features in evil undertones of light that showed a great shadow where his jaw and chin jutted forward. The smoke was good. He held out the sack toward the guard and got a curt shake of the head.

"Don't use it. Chew."

They lapsed into silence after that, each using his eyes to the curtailment of other senses. Troy drove mechanically, without effort. The horses knew the route better than he did anyway.

Troy ran a hand over his face, felt the wiry beard stubble and sighed. There was a sensation of depression within him. To ward it off he swiveled around and

109

studied the horizon. Just the faintest glimmer of dawn was showing in a thin, light pink banner of light that seemed to lift the darkness, tincturing its lower edges with a pallid, unpleasant grayness. He turned back toward the road and noticed visibility had improved a little. Birds made small, drowsy sounds as they awakened in the brush by the side of the road. The coach horses were breathing steam that erupted from their nostrils like smoke and Birch Hardin's face was drawn and old and slack looking in the unearthly light. Only his deep-set eyes moved, and the clamp hold of his jaw and mouth were set in a slant of bitterness and determination that detracted from the general look of quiet good nature and near-humour that ordinarily showed.

Troy punched out the cigarette on the seat between them and tossed it down. He was hunched over against the chill, staring into the sickly morning, when Birch nudged him slightly.

"See those scrub oaks up ahead? The ones that got the boulders lying around in front of 'em?"

Troy looked, saw the clump readily enough and noticed with inner relief that, this time, the area under suspicion was on Birch's side of the road.

"Yeah. That was the second place?"

Birch nodded without taking his eyes off the trees. "That's her. Last year's hold-up spot. Don't think that one was Carter though."

"Why not?"

"Well, there were three of 'em. One held the horses. Right out in plain sight too. Two of 'em threw down on us. Lew pulled up and one kept us covered with a carbine while the other cussed a lot and threw out the bullion boxes."

Troy cocked his head trying to pierce the shadows around the scrub oak thicket. There were dark areas where a man could easily be hiding. In fact, ten men could have been hiding there and no one would be able to see them until they moved. He unconsciously held his breath, then let it out slowly, gripping the cocked .45 in his lap.

The coach moved on at its steady gait, rocking a little because of the 'hog-wallows' in the scored old road and, except for the steam of breath and the soft music of harness in motion and horse hooves striking the ground, there was no movement or sound. Then they were past and in the clear once more.

Troy glanced at Birch and frowned. "Darn! He may have suspected something at that." The thought occurred to him that Cin may have roused the outlaws in Carter's bunkhouse and sent them on to warn the renegade, or, she might have made the long ride herself, although he doubted that, because she had fear in her now. More fear than hatred, possibly. She wouldn't risk her life to warn Jeb, he didn't believe. Birch's voice brought him back to reality.

". . . one more, then I don't know what to think." He was looking up at Troy. "You don't suppose he's went and changed his mind—or—maybe, your information wasn't too good, do you?"

Troy shrugged, still frowning. "It—doesn't seem likely, Birch, although—I did get it at gun's point, in a way. Still—well, like you said, a man never knows, for sure."

They were both relieved and disappointed at the same time, and rode along in silence. Troy didn't even bother to ask where the next likely spot for a hold-up was, he was so nearly convinced there wouldn't be one, now.

111

It made his thoughts a jumble of discord, too. He had sworn to take Jeb Carter, and some inexplicable thing was thwarting him at every bend in the road. If he didn't take the outlaw, he wouldn't be able to command much respect for his failure, and, while that didn't trouble him too much, the knowledge that Tom, Ellie, and the doctor had heard him say he would get the outlaw, was plain torture.

If Carter didn't stop the bullion shipment, then how would Troy find him? Certainly he couldn't go back to the outlaw's ranch again, or to Herd's Crossing. Then how? He swore to himself. Whatever it was that was circumventing him, was doing an almighty good job.

And Ellie—he couldn't go back to her a failure in the one way he could show some atonement for all the mistakes and suffering he'd caused, and yet, by not going back, he would cause her even more anguish. Angrily he fished out the tobacco sack, curled up a cigarette, lit it and smoked in silence. Birch was watching him out of the corner of his eyes but Troy didn't see it. The guard's shotgun was lying listlessly across his lap, an eloquent symbol of the defeat he too, felt.

"Troy: if we make it through with this shipment—what then?"

"Wished I knew, Birch. I've got a reason for going after Jeb Carter. Reckon I'll just leave you and the coach there, get a horse I left in the liverybarn over there and strike out. I've got to get him, one way or another."

"I figured it was something like that." Birch said it quietly, looking straight ahead.

Troy turned and looked strangely at him. "What do you mean?"

Birch shrugged. "None of my business. You can tell

me to shut up if you want to. It's—Ellie, isn't it?"

Troy's head raised a little, challengingly, then lowered again. He nodded. "Yeah; Ellie and Tom. I owe 'em that, Birch. Owe 'em more, actually, because I've caused 'em so much grief, but especially after Carter downed Tom, I owe 'em his hide nailed to a tree."

"I understand, Troy. But—you weren't doing Ellie any favor going up against Carter. You're no match for him."

"I know that too, but it's got to be that way. Got to."

"Yeah," the guard said slowly, thoughtfully. "I reckon. Man sure can get himself into a jackpot every now and then, can't he?"

Troy nodded, was going to say something when the horses slacked off a little, seemed uncertain, then stopped by simply snorting softly and refusing to go on. He scowled down at them, Dipped the lines gently and got another balky refusal. Birch leaned far over, staring down at the road in front of the leaders.

"Hell; there's a crack in the road there, Troy. Must have been an earthquake—or something. See it?"

Troy stood up and stared down. He could see nothing. Gentle, insistent backward pressure on the lines made the horses ease off and back up a little, then he saw it. A thin slit about six inches wide, sharp ended and dark looking. He was standing like that, puzzling the thing out, when Birch steadied himself and stood up beside him.

"How will we get over that?"

"Can't," Troy said. "Got to go around it." He looked over the range on both sides of the road—and froze the way he was.

"Hell!"

It wasn't said loudly, but Birch understood in a flash,

113

and was helpless, his shotgun was lying on the seat behind him. The lean, tawny shadow moved out into the pale light and both men on the coach felt their stomachs go cold. Prepared as they had been, wary and careful and keyed up for offensive defense, they had been caught flat-footed after all.

The shadows stayed behind, in place, when the man came forward. Bad light glinted softly off his two guns. His face was shielded by a beard except for the sunken, blazing eyes that held them motionless.

"Set the brake, loop the lines and toss your guns down!"

Troy's blood was fiery and racing so that it obscured his vision. There was no alternative. A kind of sickness swept over him. Weariness and sickness combined. Warned, knowing and prepared, aching all over from the arduous ride and punishment he had given himself unstintingly to forestall this very thing, he had been caught as flat-footed as though it had been the surprise Jeb Carter still thought it was.

Both he and Birch obeyed. There was no alternative except suicide, and that wasn't sensible. Troy kicked the long-handled foot brake forward to set the brakes. He leaned forward and looped the lines without looking down at the outlaw, then he took the six-gun from its holster and let it fall beside the near front wheel.

It took Birch longer. He had his six-gun, the shot gun, and the carbine lashed to his side of the seat in a saddle boot. Troy counted the dull landing thuds, three times, then he turned and looked down at Carter. The bandit hadn't moved. His face was turned upwards in apparent doubt and wonder, then he spoke.

"That you Troy?"

"Yeah, it's me."

"The devil! What you doing—here?"

"You mean alive, Jeb?"

The thin shoulders rose and fell. "All right I paid a hundred to the boys that were supposed to have killed you."

"Lost money, didn't you?" There was no taunt in the words. Troy's voice, like his brain, was beyond that.

"I reckon," it came out slowly. "What got you to drive this stage, then?"

"Wanted to see you again."

The outlaw's eyes widened a little. "What made you sure you would?"

"Cin told me where you were tonight."

"You're a liar!"

Troy shook his head. "No I'm not. I talked to her last night at your ranch. The place they call your hideout over by Herd's Crossing. Want me to tell you how you get there?"

Carter was motionless, then he walked easily forward and stopped where he could see Troy's face better in the weak light. "No; just tell me who told you how to get there?"

Troy shook his head. "Sorry. It's no secret around the Crossing anyway, Jeb. You're quite a celebrity over there."

"All right; tell me this then, if you talked to Cin. What was she wearing?"

"Sure. She had on a white dress, sort of long in the skirt. Lacy looking outfit with a lot of little holes in the cloth. Satisfied, Jeb?"

Carter's jaws bulged. The flame in his fierce eyes glowed, but he said nothing for a full minute, then he holstered one gun and jerked toward the ground with the other.

115

"Get down you two. You there—guard—you come over Troy's side too. No foolishness, now."

Troy climbed down stiffly and Birch followed. On the ground, Jeb Carter walked up to within a foot of Troy and stared at him, then nodded his head a little.

"All right. You saw her, I know that. Now I know why you threw her out too. She's just plain no good." The savage eyes were cold and hard. "I'll settle with her when I get back."

CHAPTER EIGHT

JEB CARTER'S RAGE MADE HIM DOUBLY DANGEROUS. He made no move toward the coach for a long while. The one gun he kept on Birch and Troy was as steady as rock.

"Where's the regular driver?"

Until that moment, Troy had completely forgotten about the trussed up man inside the coach. He jerked his head backwards.

"Inside."

The cold, icy eyes flicked over Troy's face. Carter's thoughts may have been hidden but Troy sensed them. The bearded lips split and showed even, strong teeth beyond. "You found out about him; that right?"

Troy nodded. "Yeah."

The frosty glance was appraising. It saw the dried blood on Troy's cheek where Carver's one, high punch, had landed. He inclined his head a little. "Troy—I misjudged you, and I don't like that. Mistakes in my business are bad. Man starts making 'em; he's slipping. I never figured you had it in you—all this."

No one spoke after that. Troy was helpless before the

116

gun and knew it. He was thoroughly disgusted too, that Carter had gotten the drop on them. Disgusted and dejected.

"All right." The words were sharp and abrupt. Jeb's thoughts had recovered from the shock. "Open the door on this side and dump out the silver."

Birch made no move to obey until the outlaw's gun swung commandingly, then he shrugged with a small, stingy movement and turned a little. Troy never saw it, any of it, until the smoke cleared away.

Birch Hardin had a tiny under-and-over .41 pistol in his fist. He cocked it and fired at the same time. The two noises were stunning to Troy, who was half turned away.

Spinning wildly, bewildered and astonished, he saw Jeb Carter go backwards two lurching steps, snarl in gasping silence through his beard until the sickly dawn light reflected dully off his teeth, and fire almost point-blank at Birch.

His mind screamed for him to act but it seemed like ages before he'd bent, scooped up a gun and was cocking it. By then, Hardin's body was sliding sideways along the coach, which gave a short start forward when the horses jumped, startled, in their harness, then Birch struck him suddenly and spoiled his aim.

The shot slammed the gun back against the pad of Troy's palm. It sobered him in an instant. Brought the drama into sharp focus and added a wild sense of exhilaration as he thumbed back the hammer for a second shot, but Jeb Carter was darting for the seclusion of the shadows again, unsteady on his feet.

Troy saw him spin, level the gun, and dropped flat seconds before the slug came slamming through the cold morning and splintered the side panel of the old

117

coach. Cursing in a tense, throaty monotone, Troy fired again, then there was nothing but the echo for a moment, and finally the sound of a running horse going west and a little north, using a screen of brush and weak light for protection, and Troy holstered the gun as he turned toward Birch.

The guard was sitting up, his hat gone and dust smudges streaking the gray, drawn features of his face. He had an awry, suffering look and clung to his right arm with small, rocking motions, staring after the fleeing outlaw. Curses and blasphemies tumbled hoarsely from his lips.

"Where's the thing, Birch?"

Troy knelt closer, squinting. Hardin turned back with blank, agonized look. "Here. My arm."

Troy used his knife to cut away the levi jumper and sleeve. The sight made him gasp, then clamp his teeth over the welling sickness that arose within him. The arm had been shattered at the elbow. Troy talked more for his own benefit than for the guard's.

"Hold still. This—here's a—curcingle. There's another name for it but I—can't think of it. It'll—"

"Tourniquet," Hardin said through clenched teeth, watching Troy's face with a singleness of purpose that avoided the ruined arm purposefully. "Stop the blood."

"Where'd you get the gun, Birch?"

Hardin's glance assumed depth and focus gradually. There was something like scorn in the look he bent on Troy, who didn't look up from his bandaging chore.

"Always carry one. On the job I'm a darned arsenal. Doesn't look too good on a guard's record; too many hold-ups."

"You darned fool," Troy said harshly. "Did you forget your guarding days are over?"

118

"No; but a man don't forget his training that easy, either." Birch made a ghastly smile. "Instinct. Anyway—I know my guarding days are over—now. That thing'll heal stiff, like a mule shoe." Then he swore again, luridly and hopelessly. In part it was fury, in part a suffering man's closest substitute for a strong jolt of whiskey.

"You hit him, I think."

"Think!" The guard showed his teeth. "I darned well know I hit him. Not hard enough though. Couldn't miss at fifteen feet—could I?"

"Reckon not—but he did." Troy headed off Birch's scathing and obvious reply instantly. "The other shots—after he winged you. He missed with 'em."

It was a sickening job badly done, but the flow of blood stopped and Troy helped the tight jawed guard back on the box, turned the stage around and pulled up with a frown.

"I hate to ask it, Birch, but d'you reckon you could tool 'em back to Bannock? I want to cut out a horse and take after him."

"Guess so. All I ask is that you bring me back both his guns. You'll have to kill him to get them. I want to know for sure, he's dead."

Troy was going down over the side when he answered. "You'll get someone's guns. His or mine." He went along the horses, who eyed him in frank wonder. "Birch—you know these doggoned critters. Which one's broke to saddle?"

Hardin answered without hesitation and a short, oblique nod. "That near wheel horse, Troy. He's the hostler's pet when he goes after 'em in pasture. Toss the harness inside."

Troy was mounted bareback in a short time. He

slouched, looking up at the guard, reading the waves of hell's-fire that were burning through the wounded man, in unison with the almost unbearable agony that emanated from the gory, twisted thing that had been an arm, and now lay in his lap.

"Adios, partner. If you're up to it after you're back, tell Tom about his new deputy, and have Carver locked up—will you?"

"Done, Troy." Birch lifted the lines, slacked off on them a little and nodded. "Take care of yourself. Like I told you—you're no match for him."

Troy was riding away into the new day, studying the dry ground with its deep, scarred imprints of the gunman's running horse, when Birch Hardin tooled the stage back over the road toward Bannock, cursing again in a steady monotone that left spittle on the outer corners of his ashen, twisted mouth.

The trail wasn't hard to follow. What increased Troy's perplexity though, as he loped along on the heavily muscled, sturdy harness horse, was the fact that Jeb Carter wasn't riding toward Herd's Crossing at all. He seemed to be making a huge circle, some way, that would eventually end—if it was ever completed—not far from Bannock.

He rode unmindful of the head of heat, the sun had finally managed to bring into its daily assault against the world. The sudden appearance of two more sets of horse prints beside the outlaw's sign, made Troy rein up warily. He was puzzled more than ever by this addition to Jeb Carter's flight.

It was more than a chase after a wounded killer now. The additional tracks meant the renegade had allies riding with him. The sign was clear that these new arrivals were friends, from the way they stayed in close to Carter, and were riding as fast as he was.

He looked around for landmarks, became adjusted and rode toward a small slope that ended along a bony ridge of land that commanded fair visibility from its vantage points.

The land was dead and still as far as he could see. It was strange, to Troy, that Carter and companions weren't in evidence. Bannock lay in the distance, a sawtooth outline of human creation erupting upon a plain of otherwise primeval sweep and grandeur.

He stared thoughtfully at the town, speculating. It would be imperative that both Birch Hardin and Jeb Carter seek medical care. How soon, for Jeb, depended on how hard he was hit.

The big horse's back was oily with sweat. Troy could feel it working through his trousers and recalled a blistering he had gotten once, when he was a boy, from such galling. Shrugging, he rode down off the land swell, cut in wide circles for the renegade's trail, found it finally and went on more slowly, for the sun was a ferocious, leeching object that drained man and beast alike.

It was directly overhead when he cut on to the stage road above town and went into Bannock from the north end. The muscles between his shoulder blades worked jerkily. A roar from within a building might end his life at any time. He knew, then, that Jeb had been badly wounded. He also knew that somewhere, the killer lay suffering, either under the doctor's care, or awaiting it.

Dark eyes slitted and animal like, he rode on through town until he came to Ellie's house, swung down ignoring the surprised stares he received and stumped across the plankwalk, through the little gate and up to the door.

Ellie looked up with heartrending, writhing anxiety moving the light that shone constantly in her eyes. "Troy! Oh, darling." She pulled him inside and seemed to fall up against him. He thought how naturally, how perfectly and blissfully and sort of preordained, it all was, then he spoke over her head, looking toward Tom's bedroom door.

"The doctor here, Ellie?"

She shook her head against his chest and said nothing. He felt the tiny spasms that shook her. The old gentleness flared up again. The longing to suffer for her.

"He been here today?"

"Yes. Every day, Troy. He was here until about an hour ago."

Troy was stiffening. She felt it and wondered, and held all the tighter to him.

"Just left?"

"Well, someone came after him. A man I've never seen before. They went away to—"

"Would you recognize the man if I described him to you, darling?"

She looked up quickly. "Yes, dear. He—was one-eyed and—"

"That's enough."

Ellie's face set into an unbecoming, frightened mask. He couldn't know it was because of the look that spread out evenly and inexorably over his own features.

"You—know him, Troy?"

He nodded. "Yes. He's one of two men I saw in a bunkhouse over at Herd's Crossing. Jeb Carter's men."

"Darling—" She stopped and pushed her arms up his body until they were atop his shoulders, then her fingers closed brutally and dug into his flesh. "Oh, Troy—my darling—please don't go any farther with this. God has

122

kept you and Carter apart, up to now. For me, Troy, he has saved you. Listen—Tom's much better. He'll be—all right, in another few months. The doctor says so."

She shook him gently, trying to make him look down into her face. He did, but the fire was still there, in his dark eyes.

"Troy—I—we—thought you were dead over at the Crossing. A man over there wrote Tom you had been shot and were at his house. I—died a thousand deaths, Troy—please—please—don't make me suffer any more."

The desperation made her voice soft, husky and low. He pulled his eyes away, thinking bitterly of all the anguish he had caused her, even before Carter came into their lives. Then he thought of the wide, glassy-eyed look of Birch Hardin, and the hopelessly shattered arm—and Tom, too. He sighed.

"Ellie—you don't deserve this. Never deserved any of it. And—I love you so, Ellie. So awfully much."

A hollow, dry voice interrupted them. It was Tom Buffum, a badly emaciated, weak, thin and drawn out Tom Buffum, leaning in the doorway of his bedroom, the shakiness of his legs visible through the long nightshirt he wore. The voice was as solemn as the unblinking eyes that regarded them.

"It's a thing called honor, Ellie, dear. Don't try to understand it. Just wait a little longer—and pray."

Troy felt horror at the look of Tom and fought valiantly to keep it from his face. He nodded at the sheriff, still holding her close, then he let his hands drop away. The pressure of her body moved slightly until daylight shone between them.

"Tom—it was close, a couple of times. Today'll finish it. Was Birch here?"

"Yeah. Looked like a stuck hog. Loring Campbell's locked up. I don't know that it was wise, but at least it's done. Do you think he's tied in, Troy?"

"No. Not that way—not with outlaws. He was working a different deal. One to discredit me and keep the stage line for himself." He shrugged. "I'll buy his interest out as soon as these—other things—are taken care."

"Where's Jeb?"

"That's why I came here. Jeb's wounded. I trailed him to Bannock, only he's picked up two friends along the trail. He's evidently in need of a doctor. That's why I was looking for the doc. Jeb'll be close."

"Two others—Troy?" The tight way she said it and the mirrored look of despair, nearly hysterical hopelessness, that was in her face, hurt him when he nodded at her.

"Yes. One was the man who was here. The one-eyed gunman. I haven't anything more than a vague idea who the other one was. There were two men in Jeb's bunkhouse—like I told you."

Tom's face was acquiring a rusty flush. The quaking of his legs was becoming more pronounced. It was evident only iron will held him up at all.

"Troy—I sent a couple of boys over to the Crossing to bring you back in a buggy. Hombre over there wrote—"

"I know. Ellie told me. Carter had me ambushed. He and Cin, I think." He elevated his head and showed the pale, anemic looking scar under his jaw. "That was one. Another went into my back. That's all."

"Yeah," Tom nodded, drily. "That's all. Listen—you'd better—"

"Rope it, Tom. You know better."

124

The silence between the three of them was thick with poignancy and understanding, then Tom nodded again, but said nothing. His eyes fell on Ellie; their look softened considerably. He looked thoughtfully at her for a while, then moved his head backwards, toward the bedroom behind him.

"Give me a hand, Sis. I got this far and used up the return power, I'm afraid."

She turned and looked at him anxiously. Troy forced his eyes off her handsome profile, glanced once, in gratitude, at Tom, then walked out of the room, back into the blazing sun. The thought occurred that what he was paying for one chance at happiness, was a tremendous price. More than life, maybe.

Bannock was like a ghost town. Troy could sense it because he knew this village and its pulse, almost as well as he did himself. It was the town's tension. A premonition that was felt, almost smelled, rather than seen or heard. He smiled crookedly to himself. Leave it to Bannock to ferret out that Jeb Carter was in town and Troy Muller was hunting him.

I He stood wide legged, grimy, blood streaked with an aching, throbbing shoulder. Dirty and disheveled and moving in a world of vengeance and violence all his own. It set an aura over him.

The dark, wide-eyed glance raked over the town. Somewhere, Carter's henchmen would be watching. If they had seen him ride into town, and hadn't been able to risk a shot, still, they'd know he was here—and why. He spat, deliberately stood in the middle of the plankwalk and let contempt for the bandits course through him as he made a cigarette, lit it and exhaled into the hot, still air.

He could hunt him down like a rat, or he could take

the middle of the roadway and challenge Carter after the custom of the time and place.

No gunmen, his chances against the outlaw alone, without the other two, were next to nothing. Three against one was suicide, and yet—like Tom had said—there was a point of honor, too.

Troy stepped off the plankwalk, walked out into the middle of the road and stood there, filtering the sights of Bannock past his eyes and into the sharpened instinctiveness beyond. There were the drowsy, tail switching horses along the road, tied and languid at the hitchrails. The almost deserted plankwalks. The scattered, masculine watchers who had long since seen him ride into town. Busy with their minds and mouths, knowing what was ahead, because the smell of gunsmoke and death was in the air. Then he saw the man sitting just inside the liverybarn door on a tilted back chair. There was a shiny old carbine athwart his lap. Troy's mouth was dry and acid tasting when he saw the one white swathed arm that clung to the man's chest like an infant. The flood of gratitude and affection welled up into his throat. Birch Hardin was all wool and a yard wide. If he wasn't, the gnawing agony that must certainly be inside him, would have put him down on his back, but it hadn't. That was Birch up there, partially hidden inside the liverybarn, waiting. Gritting his teeth over racking pain—and waiting.

Troy felt a thousandfold better. He straightened, pulled out Tom's gun and cocked it, then began his slow walk down the roadway where traffic, like everything else in town, then, was holding its breath; unmoving, frightened and thrilled and rigid, all at the same time.

Troy's rationale told him the outlaws wouldn't be at the doctor's house, but he wondered. Again, it would depend on how badly Carter was wounded. He kept going, hearing the dull, dust-muffled sound of his own boots in the dirt, heading toward the doctor's cottage. Every sense was bent toward the acute, fearless scrutiny for movement. Past the Palace Bar, past the mercantile, down the twin, warped and uncared for rows of buildings until he was fairly close to his objective. Through the fly infested air with its everlasting smells, neither pleasant nor unpleasant, noticing nothing; just waiting for the movement that must come, sometime.

Close enough to see the curtains inside the closed windows. Knowing and conscious of his failures in anticipating the outlaw's movements before. His confidence shaken more by this providential destiny that always seemed to save Jeb Carter at the last minute. Or save the untutored gunman who was out to kill him.

When it came, however, this time, Troy was prepared. It was a slight, almost imperceptible movement of a curtain at the side of the doctor's house, where one window was open. It was ample warning to a man concentrating as Troy was, because there was no air or movement anywhere else. Just that one small, frantic flutter—and the finger of steel with its eyesocket of darkness that was the dead end of a rifle barrel.

Troy went sideways fast, bringing the pistol to bear. The rifle spat its lethal bullet and jerked wildly when an unseen hand levered it. Troy's shot smashed the sill. Split it into three flying pieces of dry-rotting wood that sounded like steel ball bearings dropping on glass, when they slammed up against the siding. Then the rifle was bearing again and Troy was moving in fast, cat like and weaving, sideways and exhilarated. All past doubt gone in an instant. Just the primitive urge to kill, gripping him.

His second shot drew a finer line. Went into the wisp of curtain that formed a vertical line barely visible inside the opening, then the rifle coughed again, but it was dropping when it went off and the bullet plowed a streamer of dust in front of the big man's boots as he hurtled over the short distance and went face on into the yawning opening, gun arced high and ready.

The man was rolling in agony, pressing his hands over a freshet of blood that gushed from the torn, ruptured flesh. He groaned and unlocked his teeth, swore thickly at Troy's head and shoulders in the window.

Troy saw the hand, slippery and claw like, go for the hip holster. His aim wasn't good, but a miracle put the third shot squarely between the man's eyes. The head went back easily and the neck muscles uncorded, letting the unbearable suffering die with the man's soul.

Troy vaulted into the room. No full realization was in him of what he had done. Immediately a gun blasted at him. There was a mule-kick effect that staggered him back into the room, drove him to his knees despite heroic efforts to hold his feet, then he was down just as the second shot thundered out of the stillness beyond. Somewhere, a long way off, came back a soft, musical tinkling like the falling of glass. Troy saw the wide stain spread on his upper leg and felt the barest twitching of pain, then he forced himself upright again and stood scornfully, wide legged. The vision beyond, in the shade of a room where the blinds had been drawn, was of a wild pair of eyes in a bewhiskered, cruel face out of which shone the dull silver of large, white teeth.

Troy's gun was low, cocked and comforting even as he looked into the barrel of Jeb Carter's gun. The outlaw was propped up on a mussed bed where small strips of torn cloth lay at scattered random. The killer's gun was being held by both hands, and then it wobbled.

In the split second it took for Troy to see and understand these things, his finger was tightening around the trigger. When the gun went off it was a second or two before Jeb's pistol exploded, then savagely out of hands no longer able to hold it.

Carter's breath came out in a long gasp that was loud enough for Troy to hear distinctly. The man's fierce, icy eyes were wide in astonishment. He stared at Troy, who was walking stiffly toward him. Dimly, he saw the gun coming up again and felt inwardly at peace as he sensed its purpose. At peace for the first time in so very long, that his lips twisted upward a little and lent a smile to his features.

Troy's shock was gone. The leg wound was like fire, but Jeb's smile held him at the foot of the bed, unable to pull the trigger. He watched the lean, tawny chest rise and fall unevenly, raggedly, and never saw the small purple hole low, under the outlaw's right eye, hidden as it was by the mass of dark whiskers. Then reaction set in. He turned away, feeling faint and ill, and went shuffling down the hallway, out into the parlor and beyond, to where the door was hanging slack because people had just fled blindly out of it.

The sun slashed at him when he was beyond the gate of the doctor's house and standing, weaving drunkenly, on the duckboards. It was like a heliograph signal trying to tell him something. It annoyed him too, with its brilliance, so he shook his head like a hurt bear, and turned back toward the Buffum's house again.

Bannock was completely deserted, so far as the eye could see. Silent as a tomb and as still as death. Troy holstered the gun and ground his teeth against each step he took, and inside was the dull, unpleasant knowledge of triumph that cleaned his slate—partly.

He thought that, all else he could do now, was make it up to Ellie in the years ahead, and this was not so much a resolved promise, but a yearning desire, with him.

Bannock was emerging a little. Men called soft encouragement to him as he went by. He smiled a little. Campbell hadn't been able to destroy the respect every man felt for a really brave man who would go up against odds like he had faced—no matter what else they thought of him.

He remembered Birch Hardin and stopped, turned awkwardly because the blood was running into his boot now, making his footing unsure, and glanced back. The guard was standing outside the liverybarn now, spraddle legged and cold eyed, looking down toward him with a ghastly smile. The man's words came easily the full distance because of the unearthly silence of Bannock.

"You did it alone, Troy. That's the way you wanted it—I know." The smile widened bitterly. "But—I'll go in and collect his guns, anyway. Bravo—partner; bravo."

Troy smiled back. "That's the cleanest—shirt—I ever saw, Birch."

The guard nodded, still making no move and gripping the carbine in his one good fist, fully cocked. Troy wondered a little, then nodded again, turned back and walked five more steps before he was halted by the apparition of wild hatred that paralyzed him and brought back clarity of mind in an instant.

"What they couldn't do—I can!" She was erect and stiff with a face made hideous by contortions of unreasoning madness.

"Cin!"

130

"You killed him!"

"Yes—Jeb and the one-eyed hombre. Killed both of 'em." The tightness of his voice indicated full acceptance that he couldn't—wouldn't—draw against the six-gun she cocked even as he watched, and held steady in one talon-like hand, skewering him at the third button level of his shirt, with its ugly, deadly snout.

She smiled at him. "Jeb—said—you had a charmed life, when we met him after your guard shot him. I wonder, Troy? Is it a charmed life, or one that's been saved for the one person who really has reason to take it from you?"

He noticed how her level gray eyes were flaming out at him insanely, and wondered—marveled—at the awful, corrosive change that occurred within her, in so short a space of time. He sighed, feeling sorry for what was to happen because he wouldn't ward it off, and thinking of this final catastrophe that was about to bring Ellie's world down in a stunning collapse, when she pulled back the trigger.

"Cin—there's little time to say anything, and less to say. It wasn't just Jennings; it was all that long string of yesterdays without the love—with the contempt—and finally the real you, coming out and despising the man you were married to. Hating him so terribly you couldn't even pretend, any longer. I'm—sorry, Cin—in a way, it isn't you looking into the gun barrel, not me."

"Yes—I can imagine," she said, tightening her finger on the trigger until the joint showed pink-white.

"No. Not for the reason you think. Not for revenge, Cin, but because death's the only release for you—for all the warped, insane hatred within you. I'm sorry."

The surprise was complete, for the gun-blast came from across the road. It was a deafening, reverberating explosion that made him wince and lunge sideways, thinking it was Cin's gun, then he saw her hand rock back and felt the brush of death—and she was staggering backwards, staring bewilderment at him before she collapsed.

He turned, saw Birch Hardin throw the carbine down and turn away on unsteady legs and lean up against a store front.

Troy was standing like that when two strong hands groped along his chest, tightened and held to his sodden shirt, and tugged at him.

"Troy! Troy! Oh, my darling—you're—hurt."

He let her lead him along toward the Buffum house, seeing the sun dance off her hair. The sickness lightened a little. He put an arm around Ellie's waist and closed his eyes against the horrible yesterdays that lay behind them all—now.